Our Tennessee Waltz

Of Mice and Kids in Oak Ridge

Our Tennessee Waltz

Of Mice and Kids in Oak Ridge

Betsy Perry Upton

Our Tennessee Waltz
Copyright ©2014 Betsy Perry Upton

ISBN 978-0-692-27371-5
Published by BookLocker.com, Inc., Bradenton, FL.

Cover design by Betsy Perry Upton
Book Interior by Robb Thomson

Printed on acid free paper.

BookLocker.com, Inc. 2014

The cover photograph shows a prefabricated type "D" cemesto house exactly like the one the author and her family lived in. Cemesto was a sturdy lightweight composite building material made of sugar cane fiber, asbestos, and cement. At the time, the problems with asbestos were unknown. Three thousand houses were built. Each one took only two hours to put up! One house was completed every thirty minutes.

This book is dedicated to my husband, Art, and my three children, Rebecca, Melissa, and Brad, who danced this Tennessee waltz with me.

Contents

Preface

Oak Ridge, Tennessee, the Atomic City, what kind of a town would that be to live in? I can still remember when my husband, Art, telephoned me long distance to say that he had accepted a job as a research associate in the Biology Division of the Oak Ridge National Laboratory. I could hear the excitement in his voice as he spoke about his interview, "I'll tell you all about it when I get home tomorrow." As we hung up the telephone, I knew that we would be moving to a part of the South I was not familiar with.

All I knew about Oak Ridge was that the town and the laboratory were secretly built in 1942 for the purpose of producing enriched uranium for the first atomic bombs to be used in war. The site ultimately comprised about 59,000 acres, and was built on land taken from the families living there, mostly on small farms. They were told that this was for the War Effort. The residents were paid for the land, but far less than its true value. Some 1,000 families were displaced, and many of them given only a few days to collect their belongings and move away.

Then, thousands of young men and women were recruited to come to work and live in a secret city without being told where it was, or what kind of work they would be doing. There was tremendous urgency about the project, since it was feared that the Germans might develop atomic weapons before we or our allies could. Secrecy was essential, and the new workers soon discovered that once they began working in Oak Ridge, their job security depended on never talking about their work, and never asking anyone else questions about what went on in the various laboratories behind the security fence.

Now it was 1951, nearly ten years, later and Oak Ridge had become a major center for peacetime research.

When we moved to Oak Ridge, we soon learned that there was an ongoing tradition of never asking anyone about his or her work. During the nearly 20 years that Art and I lived there, I had no idea what most of my friends' husbands did, nor which of the various laboratories they worked in. The careful security in the town was graphically demonstrated to me, several times a year, from my kitchen window, which looked out on the street. Two or three times each year, I used to see a pair of young men dressed in dark suits and fedoras walking down the sidewalk on our street. We all knew that they were either young Mormon missionaries or FBI agents, since nobody else dressed that way. If they stopped at every house, they were missionaries. However, if they skipped one house and went to all the others along the street, it was obvious that they were F.B.I. agents asking questions about the residents of the house they had just skipped. Once, when our house was skipped, I was somewhat concerned, because one of our neighbors seemed to be going through some sort of emotional breakdown. Even though she was formerly my friend, now she would not speak to me. I wondered what she might say to the investigating F.B.I. agents.

During the years Art and I lived in Oak Ridge, raising our two daughters, Rebecca and Melissa, and our son, Bradley, we realized that Art's new job had taken us to a good town to live in. It was a lovely, quiet and peaceful community, with good schools, fine music teachers, and creative dancing classes, plus wonderful lakes in the area for weekend picnics, as well as all of the cultural opportunities we wanted for our children. The residents in town were an interesting mixture of many different backgrounds. I used to say that we Oak Ridgers were like the "Brits in Inja," since we had created an enclave of culture unlike that of most of the surrounding small towns in East Tennessee. By the time we moved away, we had our own symphony orchestra, a new community art center, a local theater group, several dance clubs, a kennel club, and many other organizations created or brought in by new residents of the town.

In 1969 we moved away from Oak Ridge to New York, and I focused on developing a teaching career. I had no plans to write about the variety of experiences I had during our nineteen years in East Tennessee.

In the past several years, with a mixture of nostalgia and amusement, I began to remember some of the idiosyncrasies of many of the scientists who lived there. I was always struck by what a contrast they were to the stolid country people whom I came to know, the native Tennesseans trying to scratch out livings in the "hollers" and the valleys near our summer cottage. I was enriched by the friendships in both places, in Oak Ridge and down on Watts Bar Lake, where I spent the summers with my family.

When I first considered writing my memoirs about living in Oak Ridge, I planned to write one continuous narrative. Then, as I began to recall many of the experiences I had, and the various people I met, they were so diverse that it became clear that writing them as a series of short stories would be better. The result is this collection of stories that give my own personal glimpse of Oak Ridge.

Oak Ridge, Tennessee

"Ohhhh! It's just like an Army Post!" I burst out, thrilled, as Art stopped the car at a sentry post, at the east entrance to the town of Oak Ridge, in East Tennessee. The military sentry came over, examined Art's identification, and waved us in through the gates. It was a happy reminder of my Army childhood, stopping at the gate for a military sentry to check I.D's.

Art had received his high level clearance (Q clearance) so he drove down to Tennessee from Ann Arbor, Michigan two weeks before, while I stayed on to finish the packing and close on the sale of our house. It was a glorious spring day in Tennessee in May, 1951, when I flew down to Knoxville with three year old Becky and one year old Melissa. Art met us at the airport and we drove to Oak Ridge.

The drive from the Knoxville airport to Oak Ridge was pure joy to me. It was a sunny beautiful day and the perfume of the south came in through my open car window. The whole countryside was lush and green with the arrival of spring.

As we entered the Sentry gates, on the Oak Ridge Turnpike, the main road into town, I saw more similarities to Army Post life. There were rows of identical wooden apartment buildings on one side of the Turnpike. We passed a big shopping center, obviously the commercial center of town. The other side of the four-lane turnpike, appeared to be more residential, with one family houses. Like so many army posts, the houses were all the same kind of construction, obviously all built at the same time.

"Where are the Garden Apartments?" I asked Art, knowing that that's where we had been assigned to live.

"Look ahead, up on that hill against the trees," Art pointed out a cluster of contemporary looking white buildings. "I think you'll love our apartment." Art had been camping out there since his arrival two weeks earlier.

He turned left off the Turnpike up a winding street named Vanderbilt Drive and drove to the top, where he parked in front of the apartment at the end of the building. Our apartment was on the ground floor, and the moment I walked into it, I was thrilled. We had a spacious two-bedroom apartment, with an efficient modern kitchen, that looked out on the grounds in front. I noticed several mothers sitting together watching their young children play in the big, open grassy space between our building and the apartment building next to ours.

In 1950, the year before we arrived in Oak Ridge, Art decided to apply to the Public Health Service in exchange for his Military Medical training. He was accepted into the Medical School at the University of Michigan, just before World War II began, but very soon he found himself marching to medical classes as one of the Army Specialized Training Program buck privates.

Once the war ended, Art was able to continue his training as a civilian. However, it was expected that he would spend at least two years in some branch of military service in repayment for his medical school training. Now, at the end of his residency in Pathology, he knew that he was more interested in research than in clinical medicine, so the Public Health Service seemed to be a good choice for him.

He was waiting for word from the Public Health Service, when the phone rang one day. It was, Jacob Furth, a famous pathologist calling from a place called Oak Ridge in Tennessee. He was looking for a young pathologist to come to work with him, so he had gone to Washington to consult with a friend in the Public Health Service. His friend let him look over the Public Health applications they had. When he read Art's application, he knew that Art was the young man he wanted.

Art spent a long time on the telephone, and when he came into the kitchen to tell me about it, he looked stunned, and said, "You won't believe this!" He had been invited to fly to Oak Ridge two days later for an interview with Dr. Furth.

Two days later, I was waiting, anxiously to know how his interview had gone, when the phone rang. Art was euphoric! It was a dream job with a renowned research pathologist, something he had never expected to find. Both of us were delighted. I also knew that it would be good for our family to live farther away from all the in-laws.

As the first daughter-in-law, with the first grandchildren, I was the one everyone practiced on, not an easy nor always a pleasant role, especially when different members of the family had opposing ideas about how I should be living, thinking, raising my kids and even voting.

In Oak Ridge, we were happy to have been assigned one of the lovely Garden Apartments, which was the newest and handsomest area of residential housing in town. Situated high on a hill overlooking the center of town, our building looked far into the distance at the Cumberland Plateau. Behind our buildings, there was a wooded area, with clotheslines for hanging laundry. For me, one of the joys was the fresh scent of honeysuckle blooming. During most of my childhood, the perfume of honeysuckle and wild roses had been a part of my life until we had moved to Michigan. Now, I was back in my beloved South again, and I felt complete once more. I smiled to myself thinking that I would not have to fight screaming babies trying to get them into the heavy snowsuits that were a part of life in Michigan.

During the next several days, Art drove us around the town, so both of us could become familiar with our new surroundings. So much of the town reminded me of an Army post with the rows of nearly identical houses built on street after street, that for me it was almost like moving back to an army post. I was ecstatically happy. Later I was amused to discover that the reaction of the other women I met in the apartment complex was often one of dismay, even horror, at what they saw as a monotonous uniformity of the town and it's buildings.

It soon became clear how much care and attention had been paid to planning the town. Some 59,000 acres had been selected as the site for the new secret city and the even more secret wartime project that was a race against the enemy. It was a sad story, as the luckless families living in the area were summarily given six weeks to relocate, and some, even less. The land was cheap, and there were the advantages for the new research project to being near a plentiful supply of water and electricity, as well as highway and railroad accessibility.

As Art and I drove around the town, we were both impressed by the layout of the streets and the houses that had been built in such a hurry at the time of the war. The main streets ran from the Turnpike up the steep Northeastern slope of Blackoak Ridge to Outer Drive, the lovely winding street that ran along the ridge. Skidmore, Owings and Merrill had designed the layout of the city as well as the quickly built single-family houses. The streets curved around, following the contours of the land, and large areas of native greenbelt had been left behind most of the residences. Many of the houses had lots of space around them, and now, in May, gardens were bursting into bloom. Views from the houses along Outer Drive were spectacular, as one looked off into the distance at the Cumberland Mountains

"Who knows? Maybe we'll get a house up here someday." Art and I smiled. We had already decided we wanted to have a third baby, a decision we had made long before we learned that it would qualify us for a spacious three bedroom house.

The geography of Oak Ridge was uniquely appropriate for the separation of areas of the city. In addition to Blackoak Ridge, where the majority of houses were situated, there were four other elongated ridges, that ran roughly parallel to one another in a Northeast to Southwest direction. The result was four valleys, where the city had been built.

The top-secret laboratories were located behind the natural barriers of these ridges. When I occasionally drove Art to work at the Biology Division, the entrance to the restricted area required us to stop at a second set of gates, manned by guards examining passes. There was no impression of anything else built in that area, besides the Biology Division, the other main areas of research, the plants known as Y-12, X-10, and K-25 were each hidden behind more hills and tucked into other valleys, separated from each other.

Art and I lived in the Garden Apartments for about a year. I loved the companionship of the other women who lived there. They were an interesting mixture of backgrounds and experiences. Kathleen Ryan became my closest friend. She was a New York City girl, and had been a detective before she married. But when she moved to Oak Ridge, she gave up her career and had a little boy our girls enjoyed. In nice weather, we sat outdoors, watching the children play. There were lots of small children for our two girls to enjoy.

Maria Zucker was completing a nursing degree at the nearby University of Tennessee in Knoxville despite having twin boys who were nearly four. Once in a while, a group of mothers would fix picnic food and we would all eat out in the shade. On hot afternoons, I used to turn on the sprinkler and let the girls play in the water, and often several of the mothers would join us and bring their children to cool off, too.

Once a week or so, I packed a picnic lunch, put Melissa and Becky into our big red wagon, then climbed behind them, and we coasted down the long steep sidewalk that ran from our building to the bottom of the hill. There was a lovely grove of trees partway down the hill, and that was usually where we coasted to a stop. Wherever the wagon stopped, we got out, spread a blanket on the grass, and had our picnic.

As I recall that first year in Oak Ridge, I remember how happy I was. Moving to a new city, but immediately finding companionship for me and both our girls was the perfect way to avoid the loneliness one often feels after a move.

One evening, when I called Becky to come inside and get ready for bed, I suddenly knew that our little three-year old had adapted well to our new life. She began calling good night to her friends "Night, Jimmy, night, Tommy, night Susie, night Carol, BAAAAA Cahn-nee."

When she came in I asked her why she spoke that way to Connie, and looking at me very seriously, she said, "Oh, Mommie, didn't you know? Connie's from Alabama, and I have to talk that way so she will understand what I say."

A Warm Welcome

Our son, Brad, was born in May, 1952. Now that we had three children, we qualified for a three-bedroom house. Although we loved our spacious, sunny Garden apartment, we only had two bedrooms, so we were beginning to feel crowded with three young children, one a newborn who was waking up at all hours of the night. We looked forward to moving into one of the well-designed, spacious three bedroom houses that were so sought-after in Oak Ridge.

When Art signed up to request a three-bedroom house, he was assured that we could expect to hear within a few weeks. There were always more vacancies available in the spring when people were moving away.

While we waited to hear, I spent most of the spring sitting outside with other mothers while we kept watch over our children. It was warm, and I enjoyed the companionship of the interesting group of women who were our first neighbors in there. The families who moved to Oak Ridge came from all over the U.S.

Several weeks went by. Art was becoming upset by the delay in being assigned a house. The crowding in our apartment and the baby crying at night became increasingly stressful for him. Finally, he decided that the only way to put pressure on the housing department would be for him to resign from his job. One of his colleagues had been successful using this technique, so he urged Art to do the same. Fortunately, Art knew that he was needed in his lab, as he was a member of a team involved in some delicate research. The likelihood of his resignation being accepted was remote. Even so, it was a gamble.

His gamble worked. Art's boss was dismayed by the possibility of losing a member of his research team, so he immediately put pressure on the housing department. The following day, Art came home to say we had been assigned a house.

We were delighted with our spacious three bedroom "cemesto." That was the word commonly used by Oak Ridgers when referring to the houses built during the war. The houses were built out of prefabricated wall panels named "cemesto." Surrounded by trees, the house was set back from Pennsylvania Avenue, with a nice big front yard. We had a large back yard bounded on the lower side by an extensive wooded greenbelt area with a stream running through it. It gave privacy to the houses bordering the greenbelt, as well as protection for birds and small animals. Art soon fenced in the back yard, providing a safe place for our little girls to play.

I looked forward to meeting our new neighbors, but time went by, and we didn't even catch a glimpse of them. Then late one afternoon, when I was in the kitchen fixing dinner, I glanced out the back door, and to my horror, saw flames spurting from several bushes on fire, close to our fenced in yard. I raced outside, grabbed both our girls and hurried back inside. Then, just as I reached for the telephone to call the fire department, I looked again out the door, and saw a man holding a flame-thrower.

Dressed in worn jeans and shirt, with a flowered do-rag tied around his head, he looked like a homeless bum wandering through the town. I thought, "Oh my God! There's a filthy tramp in the neighbor's yard… should I call the police? Is he going to burn their house down?"

Just then, the man he turned toward me and I saw that it was the next-door neighbor. He was mowing his back lawn by burning the weeds off. However, each time the shrubs and trees caught fire, he quickly put down the flame-thrower, grabbed his hose, and turned it on to put out the fire. I looked at the curtain of ashes floating down to cover our new sandbox and put the phone back on the hook.

As I watched through the kitchen door, I saw our neighbor move to the other side of his yard, start up the flame-thrower, and begin to burn off the weeds in a different corner of his yard. By the end of the afternoon, most of the small trees and shrubs had charred branches, and leaves burned to a crisp.

"Is he crazy?" I wondered. I had heard that Oak Ridge was full of eccentric scientists, but to me, this man looked more like a dangerous tramp. At least he was a danger to houses adjacent to his as well as to the neighborhood as a whole. What if he started a fire that he was unable to control? I lost interest in meeting him and his family.

The next time I went shopping, I bought a handheld fire extinguisher and mounted it near the kitchen door.

Time went on, and we never even saw any of our other neighbors. Then one day it all changed, and residents up and down Pennsylvania Avenue and all the side streets came to ring our doorbell.

As soon as we moved into our house, we realized that the previous tenants had not been at all interested in the yard. To Art's dismay, not only was there no grass growing in the yard, there was virtually no topsoil. Even if he could scratch into the hard packed Tennessee clay that covered our front yard, it was doubtful whether grass seeds would grow.

Once we were somewhat settled, he drove to a nearby town which had a large nursery to ask advice about gardening in Tennessee. He came home with several large bags of fertilizer, which, he had been assured, would enrich our yard, and provide the necessary nutrients for a nice lawn. Several weeks went by, before Art had time to spread the new fertilizer, but finally, one sunny Saturday, he opened the four bags, and spread the rich mixture all over the barren front yard, sowing plenty of grass seed as he went along.

"That's going to be just the ticket," Art said, so pleased with the advice the nursery had given him. I picked up baby Brad, and all five of us went outside and sat on the front steps to admire Art's hard work. "I wonder how long it will take before it really seeds in" I remarked.

"We just need a few nice spring rainstorms," Art said, assuring me that it would turn out.

Then, the next morning, we awoke to the sound of rain.

"What's that funny smell?" I asked, heading to the kitchen to fix breakfast. "Gosh, it's really pretty strong out here in the kitchen, and not what I'd call a funny smell out here. It's a horrible smell."

Art followed me to the kitchen, and we both looked out the window to the front yard. We looked at each other, and suddenly it dawned on us. "Oh, oh," Art said. "I think I'd better look at those bags that fertilizer came in." He headed for the trashcan.

A few minutes later, he came back in, looking dismayed. "No wonder the nursery owner gave me a discount on those four bags of fertilizer. It's dried sheep manure, and it says on the bag that it shouldn't be used near dwellings, as the smell takes so long to dissipate. Guess what? We're going to live with this smell for weeks, if not months. The neighbors are going to love us!"

We didn't have long to wait before we started meeting our neighbors. The doorbell began to ring mid-morning that Sunday. Everyone who came by commented that nobody could figure out what the terrible smell was caused by. It appeared that everyone was just going around the neighborhood to see if anyone had any idea of the cause.

"Oh my goodness, yes, isn't that a terrible smell?" "I commiserated with everyone as they walked in the door. "Art and I woke up this morning and wondered what in the world caused it. Tell me, does this happen often in this neighborhood?" I asked our visitors.

I crossed my fingers, and heaved a sigh of relief when not a single neighbor even glanced at our front yard. The only comment about Art's gardening work the day before came from our neighbor, the flame-thrower, the one person I did not want to meet.

"It's so nice that you like to garden," he said, looking at the rich layer of stinking sheep manure that covered the front yard.

About a month later, we had a thick green carpet of grass we called the sheep meadow.

Ain't No Woman ...

As soon as Art and I moved into our government-owned house, we began stockpiling two essentials: cloth diapers and electrical fuses. With two preschoolers plus an infant, diapers were grabbed to wipe up anything wet: a sopping baby, a half-gallon of milk dropped by a toddler, the puppy's wet feet, or the laundry tub leak in the utility room. The daily diaper pile grew like trash in a municipal landfill, and meant a lot of laundry loads to keep our heads above the deluge. With the washer and dryer going, the refrigerator would kick on, or Art would turn on his electric drill, or I would plug in the iron, and suddenly the fuse would blow. In the ensuing silence, the call to arms was not "Quick, hand me a diaper!" but "Quick, hand me a fuse!" There was quite obviously a symbiotic relationship between the two necessary items.

One day after we had lived there a couple of years, we had a major stop-up caused by tree roots growing into the drain, so we called for help from Roane Anderson, the government's emergency service providers in Oak Ridge. The man arrived and began running the "roto-rooter" machine to ream out the drain outside the house. Just then, in a fit of forgetfulness, I dumped the just-washed portion of the daily diaper pile into the drier, reloaded the washer and turned them both on. Dead silence was the result. The washer quit, the dryer quit and the plumber's roto-rooter quit.

As I reached for a new fuse, the plumber called through the screen door, "I gotta go back to the shop and git me a new snake. This one has a bad connection and it done cut out on me."

"Just a minute," I said, "There's nothing wrong with your

machine, it's just a blown fuse. I'll get it fixed."

He blew up! "Ain't no woman gonna tell me nothin' about my business! I'm takin' this here busted machine back." With a look of outrage, he got into his truck and left.

As I began to fume, I decided not to change the fuse. "I'll show that stupid jerk who thinks women don't know nothin' about nothin'."

When he returned, and tried to turn on the replacement machine, the plumber was dismayed to find that it didn't work either. So I opened the door and called him to come into the utility room. "I'll fix it for you," I said.

While he stood there, a sneer on his face, I reached up and replaced the blown fuse in the box, then told him to go turn his machine on. While I stood in the door, listening to the noise it made, I mused, "Ain't no woman can live in an Oak Ridge house and not know a blown fuse from a busted machine."

Art and I decided to remodel our house some years later, after the government sold them to the residents. Rewiring the house was at the top of our list. We analyzed our needs and decided what changes we wanted to make in the house. Then, because Art was out of town so often at scientific meetings, he left everything to me. I drew up detailed working drawings for the construction, including plumbing isometrics and diagrams for the electrical circuits so I could submit each one for bids.

The first electrical contractor to come by to give me a bid showed up after dinner one night, just as I had started cleaning up the kitchen. Art told me to go talk to him, adding, "I'll finish cleaning up the dinner dishes."

I invited the electrician into the living room and proceeded to spread out my working drawings for the proposed rewiring of the house, while I explained the changes we wanted. Then I glanced up, waiting for his comments and a suggested bid, and saw a scornful look on his face. He burst out, "Ain't no woman knows squat about wirin' a house. I need to talk to the mister."

"Hey, Art," I called, "Mr. Hammond wants to talk to you about this job. Will you come in here?"

Art walked in, dressed in my ruffled apron, rubber gloves on his hands, drying a plate as he came into the living room, "I'm sorry, but I don't know anything about my wife's electrical diagrams. You'll have to ask her to explain anything you don't understand."

Poor Mr. Hammond sat there, mouth open while he looked from Art to me and back to Art again. Mumbling something, he got up and left.

Today, I can't remember the name of the electrical contractor who did take the job, but "ain't no woman" could ever forget Mr. Hammond or the look on his face.

How to Get Promoted Accidentally

In Oak Ridge, Art worked with Jacob Furth, a well-known experimental pathologist. Chief of the Pathology-Physiology Section of the Biology Division of the Oak Ridge National Laboratory, Furth was a world-renowned scientist whose career had been spent in research, and he attracted many young scientists to Oak Ridge to work with him.

Oak Ridge was a town full of young couples, and we soon found ourselves enjoying the Harrises and Bakers. Joe Harris and Tom Baker had both been working with Dr. Furth for two years. As both couples had young children close to the ages of our girls, who were both pre-schoolers, it made picnics or barbecues more fun for all of us.

Then Art came home with the news that both Joe Harris and Tom Baker had given notice that they were leaving.

"Oh no!" I said. "Just as we are really becoming good friends. But why?"

"Tom says he just can't take it any longer. Furth drives him crazy with his constantly-changing demands, his temperamental outbursts, and, oh, I don't know what all."

"What about Joe?" I asked. "Did he explain why he is leaving?"

"Joe just laughed and told me that nobody can survive working with Furth for more than two years. He says nobody has ever lasted longer than that. One of the things he and Cindy have resented is giving up their weekends when Joe has to go back to work. He assured me that I'll want to quit in two years!"

"We'll miss them," I said, sadly.

The second year, Art's attitude toward his boss alternated between amusement and impatience. However, he spoke often of his wonderful and interesting job, and the joy of "being paid to play," as he put it.

The years went by. Four years later, Art continued to work with Furth, putting in long hours. He brought work home in the evenings, spreading it out on the dining room table. Saturdays and Sundays, he was back at the Lab working. He didn't seem to mind spending his weekends at the Lab. For our three children and me, it was a very restricted life. When Art went back to work on Saturdays and Sundays, the children and I stayed home, since we only had one car.

Then, one Sunday afternoon, in 1954, Art returned from working all morning and half of the afternoon at the Lab, tossed his briefcase down, heaved a sigh and said, "That's it! I've had it! I have to find another job. I can't go on working with Furth. He's too difficult. I'm going to resign tomorrow."

I was surprised, as Art had never said anything about Jacob being difficult. "You're going to resign?"

"Yes, definitely."

I was stunned. I just sat there looking at Art. He had always spoken so admiringly of his boss, and I knew that he had been excited about some of the research he was involved in. He and Jacob were doing a longitudinal study on the affects of radiation on mice. The animals were irradiated, then allowed to live out their normal life spans. Then, after they died, they were autopsied and studied. It was an important study, a part of the Atomic Bomb Casualty Commission, established in Hiroshima.

Art had gone along with Dr. Furth's demands on his time. He had never shown any signs of resenting the Saturdays and Sundays he had to spend working in the Lab. And, I had not complained, once I saw the way our life was going to be, even though, like Joe and Cindy Harris, our friends who had moved away, I felt angry that he had no time to spend with the family. I used to wish that the children and I might just go for a drive somewhere on a weekend and not be stuck at home waiting for Art to return. I did not discourage him.

So, Art drove off that Monday prepared to tell Dr. Furth that he was leaving.

When he returned that evening, my first question was "Did you resign?"

"No," said Art. "Furth was in Washington. I'll tell him tomorrow."

On Tuesday as Art walked out the door, he grinned at me, "I'll resign today."

Tuesday evening I asked him, "What did he say?"

"I couldn't talk to him today, there was a conference at the Biology Division. I'll go in tomorrow."

"Today's the day I resign," Art said as he walked to the car that Wednesday morning.

Wednesday when Art came home, I looked at him expectantly.

He shook his head, "Furth had visitors today. He didn't have time to see me. I'll try again tomorrow."

That Thursday, we both laughed as Art picked up his briefcase, "Try, try again…" he said, as he walked out the door.

Art walked in the door that Thursday evening, shaking his head before I could pop the question. "Furth was closeted all day with another visitor," Art said. "At this rate, I'll be here another year or two…" We both laughed.

That Friday, I didn't say anything as Art left for work. He returned early, and came out to the back yard where I was reading to the kids in the swing.

He was white as a sheet.

"Art, what's the matter?" I burst out.

"I've got to sit down. You'll never believe this," he said. "Furth called me into his office, before I could request an appointment with him. He said, 'Art, I am leaving to take another job. I want you to take over my job as the chief of the Pathology-Physiology Section!'"

"What?" I burst out. "How wonderful, Art. You'll be a great director and a good boss for everyone. But, my God! What if you had resigned on Monday?"

"My God, indeed! Just think how close I came to missing this! If Jacob had been able to see me on Monday and I had resigned, I would be looking for work somewhere else, instead of getting this marvelous promotion!"

Dr. Furth departed and Art became the director of his division, a wonderful and challenging job. Did he stay home on weekends? No. However, I saved up the necessary money and bought a station wagon with enough seats to accommodate our three kids and several of their friends on our weekend outings, so the kids and I were free to go wherever we wanted.

The following summer, the members of Art's department were enjoying a swimming party at the home of a colleague, in Knoxville. Suddenly, we all heard the voice of a man who did not work in Oak Ridge, but who was a friend of the host and hostess.

In a loud Tennessee baritone, he called out, "Y'all don't mean to tell me that flat-bellied young man is y'all's boss?"

Mountain Man

In 1955, when the government decided to sell all the Oak Ridge houses at rock-bottom prices, we renters became new owners and began a great variety of remodeling. As a result, some of the formerly drab houses became beautiful brick homes, often with elegant new entrances. Others were faced with stone, or wood siding, and many received new roofs.

Art and I were more interested in increasing the size of our house than in spending money on expensive trimming for the exterior. As it was situated on a sloping hill, we had the perfect setup for adding a full basement, with big windows framing the view of the woods below. So, we began asking everyone we knew for references for a concrete contractor. Huey Peters was the name that came back as the best concrete contractor in the area.

Then began my challenge of trying to find him to see whether he had time to add our house to his list of construction projects. He was a mountain man, with no telephone, so we couldn't call him with our request. And, he turned out to be hard to locate in Oak Ridge, since he was working all over town. Often, someone would tell me that he was working on a house on a particular street, but by the time I drove there, his workmen would tell me he had just left to go to a house somewhere else.

Then, one day in the Pine Valley Grocery store, my chase came to an end. A friend pointed to a tall, handsome mountain man at the meat counter, getting some lunchmeat. "That's Huey Peters. Why don't you go talk to him now?"

I went over, and introduced myself, saying, "Mr. Peters, my name is Betsy Upton. My husband and I want to put a basement under our 'D' house, and we want the best man for the job. Everyone says you're the best. I hope you will take us on as new clients."

Huey turned to me, shook my hand, and said, "Wah, yes ma'am, I shore kin take y'all on. Mah boys kin dig two 'D' basements in one day, so here's mah fixed price, concrete block sidin', winders 'n' all. If that there price suits you, we kin shake on it."

"Shake on it? Mr. Peters, don't you want to write up a contract?"

I was nervous about just a handshake that would commit us to an agreement, with nothing tangible to back it up.

Huey explained his viewpoint, "The way ah looks at it, ain't no contract worth the piece of paper it's wrote on. The only thing that matters is a man's word an' his handshake. If he's a crook, that there piece a' paper don't mean a thang."

Then, he looked at me and seemed to sense my uneasiness, because, with a grin, he said, "Well, now, li'l lady, if hits a contract you want, we'll jes do us a contract."

With that, he grabbed a torn section of a brown grocery bag, pulled a stub of a pencil from his pocket, wet the end of the pencil in his mouth and wrote: "I, Huey Peters does hereby agree with Mizrus......" he stopped. "What do folks call you?"

"Elizabeth Upton," I replied. "Miz Elizabeth Upton," he wrote, "to do her a full basement under her 'D' house, sidin', an winders an doors with my best concrete floor." He added that it was a fixed price job, and wrote the total price on the brown paper.

"Ma'am, does that suit you? I reckon I didn't figger on yer havin' to go home to the mister and tell him hit was jes a handshake."

"How did you guess, Mr. Peters?" I just smiled at that charming, handsome mountain man. His boys would start next Monday, he assured me.

I stopped him when he named the extremely low price, "Mr. Peters..." I started.

"Hits gotta be Huey..." he added.

"Well, Huey," I began again, "What if you run into some kind of problem and it's more expensive than your estimate? Don't you leave room for jobs that run over the estimate?"

"Now, Miz Upton, I been doin' this here business a long time. I kin tell you jes exac'ly what it's gonna cost me to dig your basement. Hit ain't no guesswork I'm doin' here." He handed me my contract, which I carefully folded and put into my purse. We shook hands, and he promised to start our job the following Monday morning.

Monday morning came and we heard a cacophony of pounding underneath the house. Huey's boys had arrived early in the morning, to knock out the old concrete block walls, and to shore up the house on pilings. They built a gang-plank for us to walk up, to get in and out of the front door. Then, the high-lift arrived, and the digging began. I knew the digging should be finished by noon, so the three kids and I sat outside, bundled up in the cold wind, watching the high-lift working under the house. It wasn't moving, but I could hear the whirr of the engine.

"We gotta put new teeth on that there high-lift," Huey told me as he returned from another job site. "Hit ain't cuttin' through like it should."

We heard the high-lift start up again, shoving against the mountain of dirt beneath the house. Five o'clock came, and Huey's men packed up their equipment. "This ain't the way it's supposed to go," Huey said, as they left. "We'll git it in the mornin', though."

Tuesday and Wednesday were both repeats of Monday. I could hear the high-lift motor as it pushed against the dirt under the house. I kept the children inside both days, as I knew how upset Huey's boys must be. Having an audience would just make it worse for them.

The following day, Wednesday, I kept waiting for Huey to come tell me that it was done. As his men were packing up to quit, he knocked on the door. He looked discouraged.

"Miz Upton, I'm real sorry. We done run into a big layer of flint rock under the house. This here high-lift cain't move it. We done wore out three sets of high-lift teeth, and they ain't moved a thang. We gonna have to use dynamite to blast out that rock. Mah boys'll be real careful, but I gotta git yore permission."

"Of course you have our permission, Huey. But we have to change our agreement. You've already lost money digging our basement. You told me you dig two D basements in one day. You've been digging three full days here, and still aren't finished. We'll go to a cost-plus contract, and tear up the fixed-price one."

"No, Ma'am!" he burst out. "We got us a fixed price contract, we done shook hands on it, and that's how hit's gonna stay."

"But Huey, you've already lost a bundle of money on this job."

"Miz Upton, hit's stayin' the way we done it in the store. I keep mah word."

I couldn't change Huey. That was the way he did business, and I didn't want to insult him by trying to pay him more. The men used dynamite for three more days, and finally, the space was clear.

I was glad to see the piles of concrete block stored in the back yard, and even happier when Huey brought his concrete mason, Johnny McDonnell, over to meet me before he started laying the concrete block walls of our new basement.

By the end of that week, most of the concrete block wall was in and two of our big windows were installed. That Thursday, I returned from grocery shopping to hear the sound of pounding. I went around to the back yard, and saw Huey with a long-handled sledgehammer, smashing out the newly built walls. Lying on the ground were the two big window frames that had been installed just a few days earlier, both smashed to pieces.

"Huey, Huey," I yelled. "Stop! What are you doing?"

He looked up at me and with a grimace, said, "Hit ain't plumb and hit ain't true, and hit don't suit me none. Mah boys knows better than to do this kind of a job."

"But, Huey," I protested, "It looked fine to me. This will just make you lose more money on this job!"

"Look here, Miz Upton," he came over looking very serious, "I don't like to lose money on enny job, but hits more important to me that I kin be proud of the work I do for folks. Mah boys knows that. If I cain't be proud of mah work, I'll jes go home and live on mah piece of land. And then I won't hafta apologize to folks for a bad job."

He stood up straight, turned to look at the wall he had just smashed, and walked away, his head held high.

Johnny McDonnell mumbled an apology to me, wiped his hands on his pants, picked up his trowel, and began laying concrete blocks again.

Johnny McDonnell's Boys

"Ma'am, 'scuse me, Ma'am, I'd like to buy me one of them bottles of milk settin' there on yer back porch."

I looked up from my front porch scan of the morning paper, and saw a scrawny little man standing there. I recognized him as one of Huey Peters' men, who had just arrived to work that morning. When they had begun the job of excavating under our Oak Ridge house in order to add a basement, Huey had introduced him as Johnny McDonnell, his best concrete mason, and told us that Johnny would be laying the concrete block to build the walls of our new basement.

That Monday was a red-letter day. After three days, Huey and his boys had finally finished dynamiting the big vein of flint rock they had run into under our house. Originally, they had expected to excavate our entire basement area in half a day, but the unexpected vein of rock had set them back. Now they were ready to begin laying concrete block for the walls, and start setting in the windows for the basement addition.

"Well, Mr. McDonnell, I see you're about to start building our basement walls. Are you sure you want to celebrate with just milk?"

"Well, ma'am, hit's like this. I don't hardly like the taste of milk, so I shore ain't celebratin'. But I done drunk a heap of sploe on the weekend, you know that's my home-brew whiskey, and mah hands is shakin' too much to lay them blocks good. A bottle of that there milk will fix me jess fine."

"No sir, Mr. McDonnell, I'm not going to sell you a bottle of milk. That's going to be my present to you. You're going to be laying my walls for my basement, so I want to help you keep them plumb and true. Tell you what, anytime you've got the shakes, you just come tell me you want a bottle of milk. We don't need to tell anyone else about this, now do we?"

Surprised, Johnny McDonnell looked at me, a slow grin on his face.

"Why, that's real nice. No, hit don't seem like nobody's gonna pay us no mind. Thank you, Ma'am."

That was the beginning of my friendship with Johnny McDonnell. At first, he only asked for milk on Monday mornings, before he started mixing mortar. Now and then, I would walk down the hill, go around to the lower level of the house to see how the work was going, and I'd stop and pass the time of day with Johnny. Or when he came by the kitchen to ask for a bottle of milk, he'd lean against the door and talk awhile.

He talked about growing up in the mountains and having to go to school barefoot. School stopped for him and his brothers and sisters as soon as there was snow on the ground. He was proud of being able to send his own kids to school all wearing shoes. "All six of mah oldest kids has gone to high school. Now, we just got the two least ones to git through school."

One Monday when Johnny came to the back door for his bottle of milk, he asked if I minded his bringing his two youngest boys with him to work the next couple of days. Their school would be closed for teacher conferences.

"Mah old lady, she don't want to mind kids no more. When them little fellers gets in trouble, she don't pay em no mind. She done got so big, she's all rolled up in fat, and she jest goes and lays down when them kids is cuttin' up. I know them two will git in real trouble if I leave 'em home. They're only eight and nine, but they got trouble figgered out to a real good system. They done got it worked out real good."

"That's fine with me, Johnny. Just bring the boys and they'll be welcome here."

The following morning, when I heard a knock at the kitchen door, I opened it to meet Johnny and his boys. I was momentarily stunned. Boys? These were his eight and nine year old boys? They looked like two of the little people from a circus, the pituitary dwarfs. Thin, undersized, with sallow faces, and fingers stained by nicotine, they stood there looking at me, more like little old men than little boys. Johnny looked on proudly when they each mumbled, "Howdy."

"Fine boys, Johnny," I said, and led his boys to the back yard, pointing out the swings down near the woods. They went racing down to play on them.

The two boys spent the whole day playing on the swings and hanging from the bars, and trying to climb the big oak tree shading the patio. When I looked out the windows of the house, they looked like little boys from a distance.

The next Monday, when Johnny came to the kitchen for his bottle of milk, he leaned against the kitchen door looking pleased with himself.

"What's up, Johnny? You look like a cat that just licked up a bowl of cream," I teased.

"Well, Ma'am, I done fix a problem pretty good this weekend. Mah boys has been gittin into my sploe, and drinkin' it when they think ain't nobody watchin'. So I tell you what I done. I wait until the wind come up and the lake gits right rough, then I give each one of them little fellers a right sizable glass of sploe, and tells 'em to drink it up, we're going fishin'. Out there in the boat, when it gits real rough, I done give each boy a seegar, and tells em, this is a real good smoke." Johnny burst out laughing, "I tell you, hit were real funny. Them boys got so sick, I don't think they'll even look at mah sploe now till they're both growed. Hit worked good with mah older boys, so I reckoned it would work with these little fellers.

"Good idea, Johnny," I said. "Alcohol is not good for kids

like your boys."

"Oh, hit ain't that. Drinkin' mah sploe never hurt nobody. Hits that them little fellers was drinkin' up my profits. But now looks like I done fix it, and they ain't drunk a drop since we went fishin'. Mah business is good agin."

Surprise!

In the early fifties, some of the wartime security was still in effect. There was a high fence around the entire area, with a sentry at each gate into town. Visitors needed proof that they were there on official business, either at the Lab or for commercial purposes. Any visitors who arrived without making prior arrangements, who had no official passes to the town, were required to tell the sentry the name of the person whom they wanted to visit. The sentry then telephoned that person to make sure the visitors were known to the potential host, and only then could permission to enter the town be granted. All of us loved the fence, the gates and the sentries on guard. It was a wonderful way to be forewarned of an arriving visitor.

It was a lazy Friday afternoon, on a hot day in May. Just before I put our three young children down for naps, I had decided to shampoo each child's hair when they woke up. It occurred to me that olive oil would be good for their hair, so I poured a generous amount into each kid's hair just before nap time, rubbing it in.

"Hmm," I thought, "my hair is pretty dry. I'll put olive oil on my own hair. We can all have shampoos." So I poured the remainder of the oil onto my own head, combing it through my hair.

After the kids settled down to sleep, I grabbed the Margery Allingham whodunit I was reading and stretched out on the chaise lounge on the porch. It was a lovely afternoon, one of those perfect spring days. It had rained all morning, but now the sun was out, and I could smell the wisteria blossoms on the vine. There was nothing on my schedule except four shampoos and a walk with the kids. They had played inside all morning, but now that the sun was shining, we could be outdoors.

Dinner was going to be the three leftover hot dogs in the fridge. I could chop them up, toss them in a casserole with noodles and a can of soup, not exactly gourmet, but one of the kids' favorites. Tomorrow was grocery day, and I could fill the almost-empty fridge.

Suddenly the phone rang and I ran to grab it before it woke up the kids.

"Miz Upton?" Asked a man's voice.

"Yes." I answered.

"This is Private Peterson down at the East Gate. They's two visitors who've come to see you."

"Oh, no!" I said . "Who are they?"

"It's your Uncle Lucius Sayre and his wife, Ma'am."

"Oh my God! Oh my God!" I burst out. Uncle Lu was Art's great-uncle, who was probably in last place on any popularity list of his family. The buffoon of Art's family, he was also unpleasant, fond of rubbing a sandy foot on a bad sunburn of any girl lying on a towel.

"Kin I do anything to help, Ma'am?"

"Oh, yes! Can you stall them for me?" I was desperate.

"Yes, Ma'am. Jest how much time do you need?"

"Private Peterson, can you stall them for at least forty minutes? I know that's hard. But…"

"Now don't you worry, Ma'am. I kin manage that real easy. I'll jest tell 'em you didn't answer, but I'd try agin. That one always works, Ma'am."

As soon as we hung up, I called Art. "Your Uncle Lu is at the East Gate, but the guard will stall them for me. I need help. Please, please go to the store right away, and buy some steaks, some salad stuff and ice cream. Three hot dogs just won't do it!"

"Good grief, my least favorite relative!" Art muttered,

and told me to take it easy, he'd get home as soon as he could.

I raced back into the children's bedroom, woke them up and dragged the three sleepy children to the bathroom. I put all three into the tub, and soaped up their hair, two of them screaming in protest, splashing water all over the floor. I quickly dried each one and threw their damp towels onto the floor to wipe up the puddles. Once the kids were dressed, I jumped into the shower, washed my own hair. Snatching up the wet towels from the floor, I used them to wipe down the bathroom, then ran into the bedroom.

I looked at the clock: "Oh no, only twenty minutes left."

I grabbed a summer dress and sandals from the closet, hid the wet towels towards the back on the closet floor, and quickly dressed. My hair was still wet, but I just ran a comb through it and put on lipstick.

Now, there were ten minutes left. I raced to the living room to pick it up. The house was a shambles, toys scattered all over the place. The kids had played all morning in two big cardboard boxes with blankets thrown over them to make hiding places. It looked as if every toy in the house had been dragged to the living room. Hurriedly, I vacuumed the rug and dusted, but only where any dust showed.

Five minutes left. The kitchen! Oh my God! I had left the lunch dishes in the sink, and the dried noodles and soup for the casserole on the counter. I grabbed everything, and just as I was about to put the dishes into the dishwasher, the doorbell rang. I scooped up the dirty dishes, the noodles and soup, shoved everything into the dishpan under the sink, then quickly wiped off the kitchen counters. Taking a deep breath, I went to answer the door, just as Art walked in with Aunt Grace and Uncle Lu.

I smiled, and welcomed them with a big hug and kiss, then took the grocery bag Art handed me and hurried to the kitchen to put the food away.

It was a pleasant afternoon. Both Art and I genuinely loved Aunt Grace, and privately believed she deserved a platinum halo for living with Uncle Lu all those years. He was a petty, unpleasant fat man with a huge belly. All of Art's family wanted to cheer when Uncle Lu fell through the boards covering the cesspool of the old family cottage on Lake Michigan. He was stopped from going all the way into the cesspool when his big belly stuck in the opening. No one in the family rushed to pull him out.

Aunt Grace was sweet and loving, and our three children spent the afternoon sitting close to her.

They left at about eight o'clock to go to their hotel. As they were walking out, I told Aunt Grace that I hoped they would come back soon. I added, "I am so glad you came to see us, Aunt Grace, but why didn't you let us know you were coming?"

She gave me a hug and said, "Well, m'deah, we didn't want to put you to any trouble!"

Sweet William

When Art and I moved to Oak Ridge, we discovered that Prohibition was still the law of the land. For us this was never a problem. Neither of us drank much except when we entertained guests. We also had a great advantage, in that, soon after we were settled, Art began making frequent trips to Washington, D.C. He was able to bring back all the whiskey and wine we wanted. In no time at all, we had a sizable supply of booze.

As time went on, and we met other Oak Ridgers, we learned that there were other ways to cope with living in a dry county. Not everyone traveled as much as Art, so they solved the problem of buying whiskey and wine by other means.

The favorite way to buy bootleg whiskey and wine, and the easiest, was to telephone the local taxi service, and place an order to be delivered. The order would arrive at the kitchen door within an hour or so. This was the favorite method of many of our friends. As one of Art's Biology Division colleagues used to say, "Hell, I don't ever intend to vote in favor of legal likker here in Oak Ridge. It's mighty nice to have my whiskey delivered jes like the milkman delivers the milk for the kids."

The second way many friends were able to have wine was by distilling it themselves. It was easy to set up a small distillery system in the house and produce wine that was drinkable, even though it certainly didn't compete with any established vintages. It was the custom to set the system up in the utility room, usually on top of the washing machine. More than one friend with a new baby used to tell me that it was a godsend having that small distillery available. Every time, they had to dump another load of diapers into the washing machine, my friends were able to have quick pick-me-ups, swigging down a couple of swallows of that new wine directly from the distillery machine.

The third way to obtain alcoholic beverages was one I didn't find out about for about three years. Then, one day, my friend Polly called. Polly was a close friend whom I had met through the local kennel club. Both of us were lovers of sporting breed dogs. She was a former well-known breeder of champion English Setters. We had become friends when I decided to show our English Springer Spaniel puppy in the annual dog show in Oak Ridge.

"Deah," she said in her charming English accent, "I'd like to drive down to Chattanooga to buy some whiskey and wine from the package store there."

"What? You mean you can walk into a store and look around and buy what you want? I didn't know that alcohol was legal there."

"Oh, yes, they voted wet in their last municipal option referendum, and now they have legal package stores." There was a slight pause, then Polly went on "but deah, I have another reason for asking you. We have discovered that Sweet William, our new puppy, suffers from carsickness when he rides with Ted and me. There is a theory that if one takes a lengthy car trip, then the dog gets over carsickness. You are the only person I know who might be willing to go along with me, and wipe our dear boy's chin, if it's necessary."

"Polly, thanks so much for inviting me!" I was delighted. "I'd love to go along with you and your new baby. And you know how much I'd like to be his nanny for the day!" We both laughed, and agreed on the date for our expedition.

The day came, and Polly drove over and picked me up. She handed me a stack of terry cloth towels for wiping Sweet William's chin, if he needed it, and I noticed that she had carefully covered the back seat with a heavy blanket.

"There's one more thing I want you to know, deah," she said as we started on our way. "The package store sometimes has someone go around the parking lot, snooping for cars that have come from dry counties. Then, after you make the purchase, and start for home, one of the owner's cousins or brothers, who is a sheriff, will stop those cars, confiscate all the whiskey, collect a fine from you, and take it all back to the store to re-sell it. We'll just cross our fingers we won't have that problem in addition to Sweet William's delicate stomach!"

"Oh, oh!" I commented. "Maybe Sweet William can foil them." We both laughed.

We were on our way out of Oak Ridge, before I turned to look over my shoulder at Sweet William, "Oops! Poor baby! He's throwing up, Polly, but I'll wipe his mouth and chin. Ok, there you go sweet boy, clean again!"

"Oh, deah! I did so hope that he wouldn't throw up at all today, and that you might just enjoy this pretty drive." Polly looked guiltily at me.

"Polly, don't give it a thought! I don't mind a bit, you know that's true... oh, oh, there you go, Sweet William..." By now, I had decided just to stay on my knees, leaning over the front seat, so I could tend to the poor carsick puppy.

The drive to Chattanooga took around two and a half hours, and Polly told me it was quite beautiful. I didn't see much of it. My trip there became a pattern: Sweet William would start to heave, I would grab a dry towel, he would throw up and I would first wipe his face and chin, and then mop up as much of the back seat as I was able to reach, kneeling from the front seat. Then each time, after he vomited, I would reach back and scratch his chin or rub his ears to try to comfort him. I certainly hoped our trip would cure his carsickness, but so far, I was not optimistic. I didn't see much improvement in his symptoms on the drive down.

When we arrived in Chattanooga and located the package store, Polly and I both went in and each bought two large bags of bottles of whiskey, gin, vodka and wine. Polly added a carton of Cokes to our supplies and we loaded it all into the trunk. She walked Sweet William a bit and then we started for home.

About ten minutes later, Polly pulled into a filling station to get gas, and we each used the rest room. No sooner had we resumed our trip, when she glanced into the rear view mirror and said, "Oh, deah! Here comes a car with a bright red cherry on top! Betsy, deah, do you really think Sweet William might save us?"

The sheriff's car whistled us over and Polly parked the car. "Yes, Officer?" she asked, "Is there a problem?"

"Ma'am, les jes take a look into yore trunk, now."

"Why certainly, Officer," Polly was her charming English hostess personality with him, as she opened the trunk. The carton of cokes was the only thing in the trunk, besides the spare tire.

"Jest a minute, lady. Didn't ya'll stop at Joe's package store in Chattanooga?"

"Why yes, officer. I bought the carton of Coca Cola there."

"Cokes!" he seemed amused by Polly's answer.

"Well now, lil lady, jest you lemme check that back seat now."

The sheriff opened the back door just as Sweet William stopped heaving and threw up. The vomit hit the officer's chin and dribbled down the front of his uniform.

"Awww, hell!" the angry officer shouted.

Polly grabbed a wet terry cloth towel from the pile already used and reached up to wipe his chin.

"Doan touch me, Lady!" he shouted. "Y'all jes git the hell back to Oak Ridge."

As we drove away, Polly and I were laughing so hard she could barely drive. Gasping, she told me she had lined up all the bottles of whiskey and wine underneath Sweet William's blanket while I was in the lady's room.

I reached into my purse and pulled out a dog cookie, "Polly, our dear boy deserves a treat." She agreed.

Sweet William was never carsick again.

In Earnest

Art and I lived in Oak Ridge for three years before we decided to look around for a summer cottage. As a boy, Art spent summers on Lake Michigan, in an old cottage built by his grandfather and his great-grandfather in 1898. When I was a child, I lived a block from Waikiki beach in Honolulu, then later on, about two blocks from the beach in South Carolina. Then when we moved to Louisiana, my family spent several holidays on the beaches of Gulfport and Biloxi. With memories of our own childhood summers on the water, both Art and I hoped to find a cottage so our three kids could have the fun of swimming, sailing and fishing as they grew up.

Several years before we moved to Oak Ridge, the Tennessee Valley Authority had built a big hydroelectric dam across an existing stream, forming a very large, and extensive lake, flooding small homes and farms but creating many beautiful new building sites around the new Watts Bar Lake. TVA then divided the available property around the lake into individual lots, and auctioned them to the public.

Art and I talked to several Oak Ridge couples who had built summer cottages in the area around the lake. Armed with their directions and a map, we drove down to Eagle Point Drive to look around. It turned out to be a disappointing afternoon, as most of the cottages were tucked into wooded lots, too far from the road to see. Besides the difficulty of seeing the homes, there were no "For Sale" signs posted anywhere. However, we decided to keep looking, as we had only seen one section of Eagle Point, and there was much more to explore.

A few evenings later, I went to a meeting of the County

Medical Wives Association, and sat next to Patty, a young internist's wife whom I was fond of. I told her that we had driven through Rockwood, her hometown, on the previous weekend when we went down to Watts Bar Lake to look for cottages for sale.

"Did y'all look at the Kautz cottage? That's the nicest one on the lake shore." Patty asked.

"No, we didn't know anything about it, " I replied.

She told me that Dr. and Mrs. Kautz had built the cottage to use as a fishing cabin and often came down from their home in Ohio to fish. Now, Dr. Kautz wasn't well, so they wanted to sell it. "Bobbie and I had hoped to buy it, but now we cain't, because we have to get Bobbie's new office set up, and medical equipment is expensive."

I thought for half a minute, "Pat, would it bother you if we went to look at it, and bought it?"

"That would be fine with us, Betsy. Look, we aren't even thinkin' about buyin' a cottage, at least not for maybe ten years or so. I'll call you tomorrow with the name and number of the real estate agent who has it listed. You'll like it, it's completely furnished, and there's even a box of Kotex on the closet shelf." We laughed.

When Pat phoned the next day to tell me how to contact the real estate agent, I said to her, seriously, "Tell you what, Pat, if we like this cottage and buy it, I promise to give you first refusal if we should ever decide to sell it."

Art and I weren't able to get away to drive down and look at the Kautz cottage for the next month. Then, early in May, he departed for the first of his annual scientific conferences, and my mother came south for her yearly visit.

I met her plane in Knoxville, "Maw, are you too tired to do some quick shopping before we go home?"

"Alright, Darling," she grinned at me, "what are you thinking of buying this time?"

"Frankly, this old station-wagon has just about had it. The brakes are uncertain and the fuel pump may need to be replaced, according to our mechanic. I've got the money saved up for a new car, so Art wants me to go look at another Ford."

"Don't say another word. We won't just look, we'll buy a car."

I drove to the Oldsmobile dealer in central Knoxville.

"Not another Ford?" Mom asked.

"Well, I'm not sold on the new Ford wagons, so I thought we'd look around"

We looked, I test-drove, and an hour later Mom and I drove home to Oak Ridge in a beautiful burgundy-colored Oldsmobile station wagon. On the way home, she commented, "Art is an unusual husband. He never seems to care how much money you spend, does he?"

"Good heavens no! He really doesn't care. He also knows, deep down, that I am the original scrooge, and would rather keep it under the mattress than spend it. Actually, he gets upset sometimes, when I don't want to spend money on something I love. Besides, I pay the bills, so I know what we can or cannot afford."

The following weekend I asked Mom one morning, "How would you like to go look at summer cottages for sale on a lake nearby?"

"That sounds like fun!" she teased, "You seem to have the itch to spend money. What's happened to my penny-pinching daughter?"

"Maw, this is a need, not a want," I said, and we both laughed.

I called to set up an appointment with Mr. Lamb, the real estate agent, to see the Kautz cottage, and quickly packed a picnic lunch. The kids came running when I told them we were going to have a picnic, and we started off.

It was a sunny, warm spring day when we drove down to

a different part of Eagle Point Drive. Periodically we could see the lake where builders had cleared off the bushes around a new cabin.

Suddenly my mother said, "Slow down, I think there's a "For Sale" sign up there on that post." As I slowed, we saw the Kautz's name on the mailbox.

I turned into the gravel driveway and stopped the car suddenly. "Ohhh, Maw, just look!" I murmured. Neither of us spoke as we sat there, stunned by the gorgeous view.

There below us, at the end of the long sloping driveway, was a small white cottage, built on the site of an old farmhouse that, later we were told dated back to the early nineteenth century. Four giant oak trees and one equally large beech tree created a dense green canopy over the cottage, keeping it shaded on the hottest afternoons.

The large lot was open, sloping down to the lake, and there were wonderful views in three directions, since the lot extended out into the lake. We could see the remains of former gardens still growing around the site of the old farmhouse, with tangled masses of unusual old-fashioned pale yellow daffodils, thick masses of deep blue flowers, rose bushes and honey-suckle.

We couldn't stop looking at the glorious views. I drove down the driveway and parked alongside the cottage, next to the agent's car and we all disembarked. "It reminds me of China," my mother said, pointing to the hills across the lake. There, on the far shore, the semi-mountainous hills, covered with thick green undergrowth plunged straight down into the water. In contrast with that view, as we looked across the lake to the left, we saw how the lake widened out and extended for miles, before it vanished around a wooded peninsula. Looking to the right, we saw cottages in the distance, and a solitary canoe making its way around a bend in the lake.

The real-estate salesman, Mr. Lamb, was walking along

the shoreline of the lake. "Well, howdy, folks. You must be Mizriz Upton," he said as he came up to shake my hand. He was an elderly man, with sparse gray hair, somewhat bent over when he walked. He wore a dark business suit and I noticed a pair of bright red suspenders holding up his trousers. I introduced Mr. Lamb to my mother and the three kids. Then he unlocked the cottage and took us inside.

The interior of the cottage was a simple, utilitarian design, with one bedroom, a bath and a basic kitchen. The big windows facing the lake made it very light. There was an oilcloth covered table and chairs set in front of a huge window, an invitation to sit and look out at the lake. I loved it, and admired Dr. Kautz's layout. It took me about five minutes to decide that this was the cottage for us. However, I didn't say anything until we went back outside.

"Well, li'l lady, jes what do you think?" Mr. Lamb couldn't restrain himself.

I carefully dusted off the remnants of my Louisiana accent, and started tentatively, "Wah, Mistuh Lamb, Ah'm jes shuah that my husban' will love this place, and would want me to buy it. But he's way out in California jes now, and I don't evah spend moh than $5 without askin' his puh'mission. So, would $5 earnest money be enough?" I let my voice drop in a tentative sort of whispery question.

Of course I knew that the usual earnest money sum was two or three hundred dollars, but I also knew a couple of cases where purchasers had difficulty getting the money back, when the deals had soured. $5 was all I was willing to lose.

My mother had moved far away from me, with the kids in tow. She was turned away from me and I noticed her shoulders shaking.

Mr. Lamb stopped, clearly shocked and gulped, "$5 earnest money?" Then he pulled a big linen handkerchief out of his pocket, and, wiping his eyes, said in an emotional voice,

"Why, Mizriz Upton, hit's been many years since I met a li'l lady with so much respect for her mister. Why, this shore is a happy day for me, to meet a lovely traditional wife like your self! Why, yes, li'l lady, yes indeedy, I think $5 earnest money would be jes fine."

Mr. Lamb and I had a handshake on the deal, and he drove up the driveway. My mother came over to me, tears rolling down her cheeks as she gasped in laughter, "You little devil! I didn't even dare look at you, because I knew I would burst out laughing. One day you buy a car and the following day you spend $5 earnest money for a gorgeous cottage!" Imitating my old Louisiana accent, Mom added, "An, you nevah spend moh than $5 without yoh husban's puh'mission!" She went into another paroxysm of laughter.

A week later, back in Oak Ridge, I ran into Dot Peterson at the drug store in Oak Ridge. "Boy, y'all sure did make a couple of enemies buying that Kautz cottage. Our insurance friends, the Harveys, have been tryin' to decide for six months whether to buy that cottage or not. Leslie told me that her husband phoned Mr. Lamb last Sunday and said that they had finally decided to buy that Kautz cottage after all, but Mr. Lamb told him that a li'l lady from Oak Ridge came down the day before and put down earnest money, and he was sure she wasn't aimin' to change her mind. They are both spittin' mad."

I just grinned at Dot, and said, "Hey, Dot, ask your friends sometime, what in the world they were waiting for."

Dot just laughed and said "Good question!"

Billy Joe

The cool breeze was beginning to warm up. The summer dawn in Tennessee is deceptive. It is hard to believe that the early morning chill will vanish as the sun rises in the clear sky. By noon, it would be as hot as the devil's anvil, I thought, reminded of the way I had been told that desert Arabs describe such heat. Now, as dawn began to break, a few fishermen trolled slowly past in small boats, enjoying the fresh wind ruffling the surface of the lake. In one, two men had pulled in their lines and were heading toward the opposite shore. "There goes Joe. He's not alone for a change." I pointed out the skiff to Art. "Makes me think of Charon crossing the river Styx, with that grim look on his face."

That looks more like the local boot-legger than a dead soul," Art joked, "though a night of drinking moonshine could make a corpse out of the healthiest ox."

We sat at the table by the window, drinking coffee, watching the mist rising silently from the lake. We could hear the voices of the children, now awake, in the bedroom. They always wanted to run down and play on the narrow strip of beach in the cove the first thing in the morning, and my answer early in the day was the usual mother's "Not yet. We'll go later on. It's too early still," this tempered with a smile.

Brad came running out of the bedroom, hair tousled and pajama shirt unbuttoned. Tee shirt in hand, he was determined to learn to dress himself. He began climbing up on Art's lap, struggling with his short legs and his round little belly, a grin on his face. "Here, up you go, Brad," Art reached down to pull him up, and settled the little boy on his lap, as we sat looking at each other uneasily.

Two days before, we had seen a large rattlesnake in the

tall weeds by the side of the kitchen door. The cabin had been empty for several years before we bought it, and the undergrowth in the neglected fields had not been mowed. I was afraid to let the children go outside now. I reached over to hug our toddler, hoping we could make the place safe for him and his sisters. We had asked around to try to find someone with a mowing machine who could come and cut down the tall grass and weeds. They were too deep for a power mower and too extensive to be cut down with just a hand sickle. One day, when we stopped to buy eggs at the small country store, an elderly man told us he would send his grandson over with his mules and a mowing machine.

"What time is he coming?" I asked anxiously, as I stood up and walked over to look out the back door.

"Billy Joe should be here soon, don't worry, it'll be all right. We can take care of the problem. Once the weeds are cut down, there'll be no place for snakes to hide. Snakes want to avoid us just as much as we want to avoid them."

Suddenly, we heard the racket of the mule team pulling a rusty old mowing machine down the road to the cabin. There was the creaking sound of the leather harness, then a voice broke in, speaking to the two mules softly as he gently pulled them to a stop, "Come on, you pretty babies, come on now. Y'all be good now, heah?"

I went to the door and looked at the young country boy who had come to mow our fields. I held my breath as I saw him for the first time, standing next to the team of mules, the reins held loosely in one hand while he gently rubbed the noses of the two animals. A shaft of sunlight shone down on him through an opening in the branches of the tree by the cabin. He was dressed in a pair of worn, faded overalls, already outgrown. Under the overall straps, the upper part of his body was bare, as were his feet, kicking restlessly at the dusty ground. His skin was dark, bronzed by the sun, his face flushed from his long walk from the valley to our cabin.

This was not the face of a poor mountain boy pinched from malnutrition, with that look of hopelessness and suspicion that I had seen so many times before. This was a face out of antiquity, a face belonging to Hellenic Greece, with a beauty that was classical and eternal. He had a straight nose, rounded cheeks and chin, and full lips beneath a wide brow. His dark eyes fringed with heavy lashes fixed on us, as he stood there. A tousled cap of curls fell over his forehead and grew long over his ears and neck. I stood there looking at him, mesmerized, ignoring the hands of my small son, tugging at my shirttails.

We went out to greet the boy and walked him around the cabin, pointing out where we had seen the snake. Becky and Melissa came running outside to meet him, fascinated by his mules and the rig hitched to the team.

The boy stood there grinning at the three children staring at him with curiosity. "Ah got me a whole passel uh little brothers and sisters, an the least one is jest about his size," he added. With that, he reached out and lifted our three year old high in the air, swinging him around, Brad shrieking with laughter. Suddenly shy, the boy mumbled, "Mah name is Billy Joe"

"My god, he's the Hermes of Praxiteles," I thought to myself, "and he's straight out of one of Murillo's paintings, as well."

My husband looked at me, "I'll show Billy Joe where to mow."

I didn't answer as I continued looking at the boy. He went behind the mules to the ancient and primitive mowing machine made of wood, and began to hand-sharpen the thin cutting blade with great care. When he finished, he took up the reins of the harness and turned the mules toward the field, walking alongside them as they began to cut the weeds.

He moved like a powerful young animal, unselfconsciously crooning to his babies, as they crossed back and forth, mowing the field. The muscles of his shoulders and arms rippled beneath his bronzed skin. As I watched him, my fingers itched for charcoal and paper to capture the beauty of this young country boy.

The children talked about Billy Joe all that day, while he continued to cut down the tall growth of weeds, delphinium and columbine, with tangled honeysuckle vines growing around the edges of the field. As the day grew hotter, Billy Joe stopped from time to time to give his two mules a rest, and while he stretched out in the shade of a tree, the children crowded around him, plying him with questions. He was sweet and gentle with them and they responded to his warmth. I also found myself looking at the four of them under the tree, pretending to check on the children, although the truth was, I wanted to keep looking at this young god-like country boy. From time to time, he looked at Art or me with a shy smile.

Late that afternoon, Billy Joe finished the mowing, and turned his mules back up the road, the children running alongside to wave good-bye.

Three summers went by. From time to time the children talked about Billy Joe and his mules, hoping that he would return, but he had left that Tennessee valley to join the Army.

One day, on a Sunday, while we were all outdoors eating a picnic lunch in the shade of the trees by the cabin, we heard the sound of a car coming down the driveway to our cabin. I walked back behind the cabin to greet the visitors. They had arrived in a somewhat dented old Buick, gussied up with white sidewalls, with a raccoon tail fastened to the antenna.

Two strange men got out of the car. The younger one started toward me, strutting with an exaggerated swagger, a self-conscious smirk on his face. He was dressed in a pair of tight-fitting trousers and a flowered polyester shirt, open to the navel, with the sleeves rolled up above his biceps. I could smell the odor of cheap pomade on his greasy hair, as he walked closer, looking me over boldly, a cigarette dangling from his mouth. Momentarily uneasy, I called to Art and he came around to the back of the cabin to see who had stopped by to see us.

"Why, Billy Joe," I heard Art say, and then I, too, recognized him. Gone was the young country boy. Gone was the open gaze of candor and innocence. There, before me, I saw just another coarse young man leering at me suggestively, like a tough young punk.

Shocked at the change in Billy Joe, I had to turn away. He continued to stand there a few more minutes, with his companion, talking about the Army, then the two got back into the car and drove off.

Afterwards, Art turned to me with a puzzled look on his face. "That was really strange. We only saw Billy Joe that one time. Why would he want to visit us? I can't understand it."

I looked at Art and asked, "You really don't understand?"

"No, it's all a puzzle to me."

"Well, I think I understand what it was all about," I explained. "When Billy Joe came here with his mules to mow the field, he was just a simple country boy, really a hillbilly, content to live in his valley. Now he has come back from the Army feeling like a man of the world. He doesn't see himself as a country boy anymore, since he has seen a bigger world than he ever knew about and discovered what life can be like outside his little valley."

"You're probably right." Art thought about it. "But why stop to see us?"

I felt a sense of sadness as I answered, "I suspect that Billy Joe felt he had to come see us when he came back to the valley because he needed to show us how far he has come. I believe he wants us to understand that now he is one of us, no longer just a simple country boy."

I turned away, my eyes filled with tears as I remembered the natural charm of the beautiful boy of that earlier summer, and suddenly felt furious,

I bent down, picked up a rock and threw it as hard as I could out into the lake, as I yelled, "A thousand curses on civilization!"

Ezra

The moment that Art turned the car into the cottage driveway from the road, the kids ran out, already dressed in bathing suits. It had become an evening ritual for all of us to go for a swim before dinner.

"The grass is getting long again," Art observed one evening, after our swim. "I'll have to mow it this weekend. We don't need Billy Joe again, with his team of mules and that big mower. But we do need to keep the grass short enough to discourage poisonous snakes and other critters."

We brought our power mower down to the cottage from Oak Ridge, and the two of us took turns keeping the place neatly mowed off for the first two months that summer. In time, however, we discovered that mowing the two and a half acres of land surrounding the cottage was sometimes challenging. Art had hay fever and I had asthma, and as the summer wore on, both of us found that the weeds triggered our allergies.

I turned to Art, "Tomorrow the kids and I are going down to Mr. Cameron's boat dock to get milk at his store, so I'll ask whether he can suggest someone to mow for us. You and I can mow it occasionally, but we really need a regular person to keep the grass short."

"Great idea," Art said.

The following morning, as we turned into the parking lot at the boat dock, Mr. Cameron came out of his small store. He greeted us in his charming Scottish brogue, "Good morning, lassies and laddies!" He then performed a courtly bow, with a smile on his face.

"Mr. Cameron, we need to find somebody who will mow our place on a regular basis. Can you suggest anyone?" I asked.

"We'll ask Willie. His family is hard-hit by the mill letting people go," Mr. Cameron said. He got up, walked to the back door and whistled.

I heard Willie call back. He was down on the dock, filling the fuel tanks on a big Chris-Craft yacht. A few minutes later, Willie stuck his head in through the door, and gave me a big grin, "Howdy there, Miz Upton." He was a skinny 16 year old with a tousled head of blond curls, always cheerful, always with a big grin on his face.

"Willie," Mr. Cameron asked, "Mrs. Upton is looking for someone who will mow off her place every couple of weeks."

"That's jes the job fer mah grandpa Ezra," Willie burst out. "The mill ain't never goin' take him back, with his heart bein' so poorly. Hit'd mean a heap to grandpa to git him a job agin."

"But, Willie," I protested, "Mowing is hard work. I'd be afraid he might have another heart attack working in this heat."

"Miz Upton, hit's a heap more important how mah Grandpa feels about hisself, than whether he dies doin' the work. If he cain't ever git him another job, he's jes gonna die anyhow, but feelin' real bad about hisself."

Mr. Cameron and I looked at each other. "Willie's a wise young man," he said to me.

I agreed immediately, "You're right, Willie. Your grandpa Ezra is just the man for the job." Willie said he would tell his grandpa when he went home after work.

The next morning, I looked out the kitchen window and saw Willie's grandfather walking down our driveway. Dressed in worn overalls, he walked slowly in the hot Tennessee sun and I looked him over carefully as he approached the cottage.

I had never met Ezra, and had only seen him sitting on the narrow porch along the front of his cabin. Chair tilted back, he sat watching his wife doing the laundry outside in the dusty front yard in a big metal tub set on top of an open fire on the ground. It used to make me angry to see him sitting there, motionless, while his wife struggled to lift the heavy metal tub filled with soapy water, onto the fire to warm up, her head covered with a scarf, sweat running down her face. When I spoke to Mr. Cameron about my critical feelings, he explained to me that laundry was considered woman's work. If a man helped his wife with the wash, he would humiliate her and demean himself. Other kinds of work were done only by the men. Only men handled mules or drove cars or pickup trucks.

What was Ezra like? I wondered. Now I saw a heavy-set man elderly man, balding, his face seamed from years of exposure to the hot Tennessee sun, breathing heavily as he came up to me where I stood in the shade of one of our big oak trees. He put his hand on the tree trunk, and gently caressed the rough bark, looking up at the huge old tree as he stood there catching his breath.

"Mornin', ma'am. Mah grandson, Willie done tole me you folks need help mowin' off this here place."

I shook hands with him, as I answered, "Welcome, Mr. Towson, we're mighty glad you can do the mowing for us."

We walked back to the pump house where I showed him the mower and can of gasoline.

"Well, ma'am, I might as well git started right now."

It was a terribly hot day, and I worried about Ezra working in that hot sun. Now and then, he stopped to lean on the mower, breathing heavily. I tried to think of some way I could get him to sit down and really rest. I could hear the kids playing inside the cabin,

Suddenly, I had an idea. I went inside and came back out with a Coke in each hand. I went over to Ezra, and when he stopped the mower, I said, "I've been working all morning, and I need to sit down and rest. Won't you come keep me company? We can sit right there in the shade of that oak tree."

That began a ritual for us. Every time Ezra came to mow, I watched the clock, and after about an hour and a half, I'd tell him that I was tired, and needed a rest, so we sat down under the tree, drank our Cokes and talked. If the mowing took longer than usual, I tried to fit two rest periods into the day. At first, we sat there, mostly in silence, just looking at the lake. Then, gradually, we began to develop a friendship, and talked a bit about ourselves, our families and neighbors.

One morning, when Ezra arrived to mow, I noticed that he seemed downcast. This was unusual. He had always been cheerful, even upbeat.

"Are you OK., Ezra?" I called to him through the kitchen window.

"Purty good," was his reply, and then started to mow.

As soon as I could, I carried two Cokes out to the field, and gestured to Ezra to come sit down with me.

He turned off the mower, but said, "I reckon I don't need no rest now. You go set a spell and I'll jes keep on workin"

I refused to let him keep working, "Oh, come on now, Ezra. If you don't feel like talking, that's just fine with me. But I'm tired. I really need to sit down awhile in the shade."

Ezra and I sat there in silence on the ground under the big tree, drinking our Cokes. Then, he looked up at the branches above us. The old oak tree had a beautiful leafy canopy of symmetrical branches spreading out in all directions. Out of the corner of my eye, I saw tears running down Ezra's weather beaten cheeks.

Suddenly he burst out, "I jes gotta tell you, ma'am, I'm a murderer. Hit's done broke my heart, but hit's true."

Startled, I stifled my impulse to say anything for a minute, but finally I said, "Tell me about it, Ezra."

He cleared his throat, and said, "Mah Ain't Mamie lives over yonder, cross the valley, back of the holler. Her place was built by her grandpa. He done plant him a whole lot of trees when he lived there. The biggest tree, was a old oak like this'n," he looked up again at the branches above us. "Hit growed out in the open, so wasn't no trees crowdin' it. Them branches was jes like a big umbrella. Folks used to stop when they'd go past, jes to look at that tree."

He reached into his overalls, pulled out a handkerchief, and wiped his eyes. "That there tree was one me and my cousins larn't to climb when we was little fellers. We larn't to hide up in them branches when one of us was gonna get a whuppin'. Our folks never knowed where we was hidin'."

"Last weekend, mah Uncle Collier come by and tole me that Ain't Mamie wanted me to come cut down that there tree. She'd pay me twenty dollars to do the job. Well, me and the missus, we went on over to Mamie's to see why she wanted the tree cut down, and her reason, hit were pretty bad. Ain't Mamie jes wanted somebody to count the rings in that old tree, and tell her how old it was."

Ezra stopped, unable to go on. He wiped his eyes again, took a sip of his coke and looked up at our magnificent old tree again. I just waited until he started talking again.

"I tole Ain't Mamie I jes couldn't cut that tree down. That there tree was like a member of the family. "Mamie jes said, 'Well if you ain't goin' to cut it down fer me, I'll jes pay somebody else $20 to do it. Hits my tree and afore I die, I want to know how old it is.'

"Then when we git home, my ole woman she jes started yellin' at me. Didn't I know I couldn't stop that crazy old woman? Couldn't I see she already done made up her mind to git that tree cut down? Didn't we need Ain't Mamies's money real bad? So, when mah grandson Willie come by in the pickup, I sent him over to tell Ain't Mamie I would do the job fer her. Saturday, I went on over to Mamie's place, and I spent all day, but I done the job. Hardest thang I ever done. All day long, the tears was runnin' down mah face. An I want to tell you, when that tree hit the ground, I hear it cryin' inside. That's when I knowed it warn't jes a old tree. That there tree had a livin' spirit inside that I done kilt."

Ezra and I sat there in silence a while. Finally I stood up, "Come with me, Ezra," I said. "I need to show you something."

We went around the cottage to the other three huge oak trees shading the cottage. There, growing under the spreading canopy of oak limbs, were two oak seedlings, each one about two feet tall.

"Ezra, we know we're all going to die, every one of us. Then the young ones grow up to take our places. You didn't have any choice about cutting down your Aunt Mamie's tree. She decided it was time for that tree to die. Now, here's what you're going to do. When you get home, go find two good spots to plant these baby oak trees. Then on Sunday, when Willie gets off work at the boat dock, bring him down here, and we'll dig these little trees up and plant them in your yard."

Ezra wiped his eyes again and just looked at me. I shushed him when he started to protest. "I cain't jes take yore trees. Maybe Mr. Upton wants to keep em here."

I just smiled and said, "No, Ezra, they're going to your place. Let's just think about it for a minute now: when Willie's great-grand-babies are about to get a whipping, they are going to be hidin' up in the top of one of these trees."

After I said this, I felt angry with myself. I knew that if someone were to cut down one of our huge old oak trees, it would take a lot more than a couple of spindly little saplings to make me feel cheered up. I just hoped that perhaps the activity of digging up the saplings, and planting them where Ezra wanted them, might at least be a way to work off some of his grief.

On Saturday, when Willie came driving the old pickup down our driveway, he gave me a V for victory sign.

"What's that for, Willie?" I asked, as Ezra walked away toward the two small oak trees.

"Miz Upton, I jes wanted to let you know, you done got mah grandpa's thinkin' right turned around. He stopped talkin' so much about mah Ain't Mamie's tree he cut down, leastways, not out loud. Now he's talkin' about them baby trees, and how we got to give 'em water and watch 'em grow big."

Both Willie and I stood there and grinned at each other. Then as I turned away to hide the sudden tears in my eyes, I saw young Willie furtively wipe his eyes on his arm as he watched the old man bend over the young trees.

Going to Hell in a Grocery Basket

"No, I just can't look another hotdog or hamburger in the face…so. What should I cook for this crowd?" I sat at the kitchen table, writing out my grocery list for the weekend, from time to time looking out the big window at the lake. The water was as still as glass on that calm, early Tennessee morning in July.

We had invited friends to come down to the lake for a picnic on Saturday afternoon, so today was the day I had to drive to Rockwood to get food for the party. But what food should I fix? As I sat there thinking about possible menus, I suddenly remembered a party I had the winter before, in Oak Ridge. "That's it! Everyone loved the Gaston beef stew I served. It will be just the thing for this weekend. A big vegetable salad to go with it, rolls, and dessert," I said to myself. I remembered my mother telling me that, in the Tropics, they always served hot food for dinner. Since Tennessee in July is also pretty hot and humid, beef stew should taste good after an afternoon of swimming and water skiing.

Quickly, I finished writing out my shopping list. "Beef, onions, potatoes, carrots, uh oh! We don't have any sherry or wine." I should have brought some from town so I would have it on hand. Tennessee was still largely a "dry" state, so alcoholic beverages were illegal to buy, sell or drink, except for communion wine. We had a good supply of wine and whiskey back in Oak Ridge since Art traveled so frequently. We justified our illegal supply as necessary to have available to serve to the frequent visitors we entertained, many of them from Europe, accustomed to wine with meals. As Art used to say, "How can you serve grape juice to a Frenchman with his dinner?"

I thought about driving home to Oak Ridge to get some sherry, then suddenly remembered hearing that cooking wine was usually available in Tennessee grocery stores. It was heavily salted, so nobody could drink it. But it was fine for cooking. All a cook had to do was eliminate any other salt the recipe called for, and substitute the salt in the wine.

I called Art and told him I was going grocery shopping and the kids were staying home with him. Then I drove off to the nearby small town where we shopped.

The drive to Rockwood was always a balm to my spirits. I drove out of our driveway, turned onto Eagle Point Drive and drove along the lakeshore. Watts Bar Lake looked beautiful, sparkling in the morning sunshine. Across the lake I could see the distant wake of a speedboat pulling a water skier.

As I passed the summer cottages along the road near our cottage, I saw that many were still closed up. Most of the families would come down to the lake on the weekend. We were one of the few families who spent the entire summer at the lake, since Art didn't mind his daily commute to the Lab to work.

Turning onto the county road from Eagle Point, I drove along the large embayment of the lake, where it lay parallel to the road to Rockwood. Along the road and back up the valley, I could see the unpainted cabins of the country people. I waved to Mamie Ebbets hanging out her laundry as I passed her cabin. The purple morning glories growing over her front porch were in full bloom.

When I got to Rockwood, I parked in front of the Quick Check and went in, grabbing a grocery basket. The first thing to locate was the wine or sherry, since, without that, I would have to change the menu for our picnic.

Up one aisle, down the next I walked slowly, looking for "cooking wine." No luck. I checked each shelf a second time, in case I had missed it.

Finally, I decided it would be easier to ask directions instead of plodding up and down aisles. In thirty minutes, I had only covered about a third of the store's shelves.

I walked over to the produce department and asked Joey, the elderly man working there, if he knew where I could find the cooking wine.

Joey turned and looked at me, his face suddenly pale and sad, "Oh, li'l lady, lemme speak to you jes like I was yore daddy. Don't you start messin' with that there wine. If you want to drink, please, you go and git you some nice grape juice, then you ain't likely to turn into a drunk. I'd jes hate to see you do that to yourself."

Mouth open in shock, I managed to suppress a giggle, then tried to explain to Joey that I only wanted to buy the wine for cooking. In spite of my explanation, he just looked at me sadly, without saying another word. It was clear that he believed that I was not only a drunkard but a liar as well.

After this, I went to the cashier, and asked her, "Miss, please tell me, where can I find the cooking wine?"

The young cashier stared at me in horror, then, looking around herself, from one side to the other, she leaned close to me and whispered, "Oh, please, ma'am, don't talk like thet." Then she turned away from me, ignoring my question.

The only thing I could think of doing was to go and find the owner of the store and ask him. Mr. McKenny was also the butcher, so I walked to the rear of the store to the meat department.

"Yes, ma'am, what kin I do for you today?" he asked, greeting me with a pleasant smile.

"Mr. McKenny, where can I find the cooking wine?" I asked.

Clearly shocked, Mr. McKenny stood still, staring at me a moment, then, his face turning bright red, he suddenly began to rage at me. "How dare you think I keep wine in my store?

I'll have you know this here grocery store is a God-fearing, respectable store. I am a Babdis, and I hope, sweet Jesus Christ, that no one will ever think I would sell wine to a sinner!"

By this time I was really becoming angry myself. I turned away from the owner, gritted my teeth and muttered to myself, "I know you sell cooking wine here, you Babdis fathead. I'm going to find it and shove it down your throat. What nerve, calling me a sinner, implying I'm a drunk sinner... Just you wait, all you narrow-minded idiots, just you wait..."

I was on my own, with only a grocery basket to shove around in my anger. Still, I was convinced that somewhere that store would have a supply of cooking wine, since they sold standard products from the major producers.

Back I went to continue my careful search. Lifting a bottle of each product, I carefully read the ingredients before replacing it on the shelf.

Suddenly, I hit pay dirt! The bottle in my hand, a lovely chestnut color, had a label of contents: "Sherry wine and salt." The salt content was, of course, very high, as was to be expected. Nobody would be able to swallow this stuff.

I looked for the big label on the bottle, expecting to see "Cooking Sherry." To my surprise and great amusement, the label said, "Newburgh Sauce." I laughed. The big suppliers had come up with a clever ruse to get the sinful stuff into stores owned by all the "Babdis." I felt quite pleased with my find. Then, I quickly filled the basket with everything else we needed, and headed for the checkout.

I asked the girl if she would please call the manager, then added that I had found the cooking wine, When the manager came up to the checkout, there was a general rush of the other shoppers to surround us, and see what might be fireworks. They had overheard the manager yelling at me, earlier, and now waited to see what would happen next.

I picked up the bottle and showed it to the manager, "I found the cooking wine I was looking for. Here it is, and you can see for yourself what the contents are: "Sherry and salt." If you look at the salt content, you can see that it is so salty, nobody could drink this stuff."

The owner reached out for the bottle as cautiously as if I had a venomous snake in my hand. He took the bottle, then looked up, and in a loud voice, said, "Why, this here is Newburgh sauce, this ain't wine. I wouldn't have wine in my store, I already tole you that!"

"That is not Newburgh Sauce," I argued, "Newburgh Sauce is a cream sauce, it's white and thick. I know. I've made Newburgh Sauce many times. This is clear dark liquid like sherry or wine. Just look at the label's contents."

The owner must have been a good poker player. I soon realized he had no intention of reading the contents aloud. He just repeated what the label said, "Newburgh Sauce," looking quite pleased with himself.

Then, in an attempt to be agreeable to a regular customer, he turned and asked me, "What I'd like to know, Ma'am, is what you was plannin' to cook, if you had of found the cookin' wine you want?"

"I want to put it into beef stew for a party," I replied.

Mr. McKenny, the young cashier and all the women gathered around looked at me open-mouthed. There was dead silence as I paid my bill and walked out.

It wasn't until I got back to the cottage and told Art what had happened, that something suddenly dawned on me. Turning to Art, I laughed ruefully as I commented, "Do you remember when we ate stew at Annie's that time? She grew up in the Smoky Mountains, you know, and her stew was made of salt pork, beans, potatoes, a couple of onions, turnips and one carrot. That's how most country people make stew. I doubt whether anyone from the country or the mountains of

Tennessee ever heard of putting wine into stew."

Art just looked at me, a questioning expression on his face.

"So now, I just realized that I gave everyone in the Quick Check the absolute proof that I am a liar, when I said I wanted that wine to use when I make stew. None of them ever heard of such a crazy thing to put in stew."

That following Sunday as I watched our guests enjoying the meal I had prepared, several people complimented me on the delicious beef stew. I couldn't help wondering what their reactions would be if they knew it had been cooked by a sinful, drunken liar.

Something to Crow About

It was a Sunday morning in July, and the family was finishing breakfast, all of us talking about taking the boat out early to water ski with our new slalom ski. Suddenly, someone began knocking on the back door of the cottage. It startled us. Eight-thirty on Sunday morning was not a time when visitors arrived, especially down at Watts Bar Lake, a slightly off-the-beaten-track corner of Tennessee, where we spent the summers at our cottage. I wondered whether one of our neighbors needed to borrow something.

"I'll answer it." Brad jumped up and went out to the screened porch to see who was there.

"Maw, Dad," he came back inside with an uneasy look on his face. "There isn't anyone there. They must have gone away."

"There must be someone, darling. Maybe they went around to the front door," I told Brad.

The knocking started again. It was still at the back door. This time, Becky got up to answer it, "I'll go." The knocking stopped as soon as she stepped out onto the porch. She came back in, looking pale, her eyes big, "Mom, Dad, Brad's right. Nobody's there. This is kind of scary."

Melissa wasn't going to admit she was frightened. "Well I'm not afraid. Mom, I'll go out there with you."

"Wonderful! We'll take a look together," I answered. The kids were right. This was bizarre. Why would someone run away and hide after knocking at the door?

Just then the knocking started again, this time, more insistently. By the time Melissa and I got to the back door, the knocking had stopped. We went outside together, walking around the cottage, and looking behind trees and bushes to see if someone might be hiding. There was no one in sight.

"Art, this is really weird," I said, as we went back inside. "It must be some crazy person. I'm going to stand in the corner of the porch, and see if I can spot the nut, before he runs away."

"It's just a joke, I'm sure of that." Art said. "It's probably Brad's friend, Jimmy, playing tricks on us."

"But, Daddy," said Becky, "If it is Jimmy, then where does he run to hide?"

I walked out onto the porch and stood in the corner where I could watch the back door. Suddenly the knocking started again, louder this time. I tiptoed over to the door, and looked out. No one was there. But then I looked down. Furtively peering up at me from beneath the edge of the porch was a big black crow. He had been banging with his beak on the door then hiding under the porch when he heard our footsteps.

Quietly, I opened the screened door. Our visitor stood there looking up at me. After he finished a thorough appraisal of my looks, he hopped up the steps, and through the door, first stopping to look around at the porch, then hopping through the door into the cottage.

"Oh, look, kids, the poor thing has had his wings clipped off. He must be hungry. He can't catch food if he can't fly!" We all looked at the beautiful sleek black bird, standing there in the kitchen, calmly looking around at all of us.

I pulled out a box of breakfast cereal, and added some of Cindy's canine kibble, which I pounded into small pieces. When I offered the food to the bird, he gobbled it down. Evidently he had come knocking on our door, hoping to be invited in for Sunday breakfast.

I hate seeing animals or birds kept in cages. By clipping this bird's wings, someone had imprisoned him in a cage without bars, leaving him unable to fly, unable to fend for himself. It was heartbreaking to see a beautiful creature of the sky tied to the earth.

"Let's keep him and feed him, and wait for his wings to grow out," I suggested to the family. There was unanimous agreement. We also agreed that we should not talk about the bird to anyone outside the family, because, if the person who had clipped his wings knew where he was, our beautiful black crow would not be able to remain with us.

So Blackie became part of our family that summer. We had to be careful not to let our spaniel, Cindy, bother him. However, after Cindy was pecked once or twice, and the crow was growled at, they developed a cautious respect for each other, a good example of a kind of political and military detante.

Blackie thrived, and bit-by-bit, his feathers grew out. We applauded each new bit of growth, looking forward to the day when our small black guest could fly away.

Then one day in late August, a pickup truck came down our drive and an elderly man got out. Art was at work, but the kids and I were outside hanging up wet bathing suits and towels, so we walked over to greet him.

"Howdy, folks. I live back in the holler down the road a piece. Some one tole me they seen a black crow around your place, so I come on over to see it. My wife is laid up with cancer so I done caught a crow and clipped his wings so's I could make him a pet for her. When he went off, she took on pretty bad, crying over her pet bird. So I come on by jess kinda hoping it's my wife's bird you folks got."

We took him around to the front of the cottage where Blackie was sitting up on the picnic table, one of his favorite perches.

"Why, that there's my wife's pet aw'right. She's shore going to be a happy lady when she gits it home agin. I thank you folks for takin' care of him so good."

The kids just stood there silently as I said good-bye, and the old man drove off.

"I'm glad our Blackie has someone who needs him and who loves him so much." I said. "We all need to be needed and loved, not just people like us, but dogs like Cindy, birds like Blackie, cats like Teeo and even snakes like Brighty."

I went over to the clothes-line and pulled our bathing suits down. "Let's go swimming again, kids."

The three of them just nodded. We swam for the rest of the afternoon without talking much.

A year went by. Then the following summer on a warm June evening, our family was enjoying supper at the picnic table in front of the cottage. Suddenly an old pickup truck drove down the driveway and stopped next to the cottage. Art and I walked back to and recognized the elderly man who had come to take away Blackie, our pet crow, the summer before. He climbed out of the pickup with a simple homemade cage in hand, and stopped as we met him.

"Howdy, folks," he said as he stood there, cage in hand.

"Why, good evening," Art answered, holding out his hand to the old man. "Won't you come sit down and have something to drink?"

"No, cain't stay. I jest come to bring you folks my wife's pet crow, seein' as how y'all was so good to him when he got away from us last year. You see, my wife done passed away, and havin' this little feller around is kinda hard for me these days. I keep rememberin' how he made her feel happy when she was too sick to do nothin' but jest lay there laughin' at her pet."

"Of course we'll take him and he'll have a good home with us," I assured the old man, as Art reached out to take the cage.

He turned to go, tears in his eyes, thanking us as he got into his truck.

Once Blackie was out of his cage, he jumped up onto the picnic table, his favorite perch the summer before. Cindy, our dog came running over to investigate the strange bird, but stopped when she saw the crow. The two had become accustomed to each another the summer before, and they would again.

"Well now, darlings," I said to the kids, "We can settle down and watch Blackie's feathers grow back."

Becky, Melissa and Brad all smiled back at me, with tears in their eyes.

Tennessee, Italian Style

During the nearly twenty years Art spent working at the Oak Ridge National Laboratory, there were many scientists who came to visit. Some came to see Art and visit the Pathology-Physiology Section he directed, while others came to participate in scientific conferences. In addition, from time to time, young scientists came from other countries to spend a year or more working with Art. In most cases, they brought their wives and children, so the whole family could have the experience of living in the United States for a year.

We always entertained visiting scientists who came for a day or two to visit the Lab or to attend a conference, usually with an invitation to dinner, or a drive down to our cottage on Watts Bar Lake for a picnic supper, if the weather was mild.

However, each time that Art welcomed a visiting scientific fellow who had come to spend a year in his lab, we tried to maintain an ongoing relationship with the young scientist and his wife. We knew it was important to welcome them as soon as they arrived so that they would not feel neglected. In order to meet each family in a comfortable home atmosphere, we always invited them to dinner shortly after they arrived. I also tried to assure the wives that they should feel free to call on us for information or help in becoming familiar with Oak Ridge and its shops. These first family dinners also helped me find out what languages the new couple spoke and if there were other languages they might understand. This was especially useful information when we invited foreign families to come and share a Thanksgiving or Christmas meal.

We usually had a crowd when we entertained on special

holidays, and I often seated people around the Ping-Pong table. Covered with sheets, and decorated with lots of flowers or greens and lighted candles, it was transformed into an attractive holiday table and it had the capacity for seating many guests.

One year, I learned that the Turkish wife spoke some German, so she was seated next to the Swiss couple. I noticed that she came out of her shy shell and was quite vivacious when she was moved away from her domineering husband. "Wonderful!" I said to myself. The French visitors were happy to be with their own small French group, but they also warmly welcomed our Japanese visitor, who had studied in France. One Greek visitor spoke some Spanish, so he was seated near any Spanish speakers. Our family enjoyed the polyglot gatherings, both on the winter holidays and on the picnics at the lake in the summer.

Once in a while, one of our visitors did ask for advice about shopping, dry cleaners, the public library, or the public swimming pool in Oak Ridge. Then, a most unusual request for advice came from a young Italian scientist, who was spending a year with Art.

Giovanni Beladino arrived with his family from Italy in the early 60's. At one of our picnics at the lake, he hesitantly approached me when I was standing apart from the crowd, just watching the kids in the water. "Oh, Meesus Opton, please, may I ask something?"

"Of course, Giovanni, what is it?"

"Meesus Opton, I am so happy to see Dr. Opton has a wanderful barber. He has hair cut like Italian haircut, very nice, not like other mens' haircuts in theese country. Please to tell me who ees Dr. Opton's barber."

"Oh, Giovanni, I am so sorry to tell you, but my husband does not go to a barber. I am the one who cuts his hair." Art walked up just as I said this.

"What? Dr. Opton, how does your wife cut hair like Italian barber?"

Art added, "Giovanni, I had a haircut in Rome and Betsy insisted on standing right next to the barber, watching everything he did. The poor barber was not too happy about it, until Betsy told him it was the best haircut I had ever had. Now, she cuts my hair the way that Roman barber did."

"Oh, no," moaned Giovanni, a downcast look on his face. Suddenly he brightened, "But, Meesus Opton, do you cut hair for other peoples? Dr. Opton has real Italian haircut, just like Roma."

"Sorry, Giovanni," Art interrupted. "We are both nude when Betsy cuts my hair, so we won't get it all over our clothes. And afterwards, I have to mop the bathroom floor!"

Poor Giovanni walked away, disappointment in every move. The following week, I suddenly had an idea. I drove to nearby Knoxville to my favorite beauty parlor. Callie, the beautiful blond owner was just putting finishing touches on a woman's hair. "Hey there, cutie! " she said. "I don't have an appointment for you today, do I?"

"No, Callie. I came to ask you something else. " I repeated the conversation that I had had with Giovanni at the cottage, and finished by asking her if she would cut his hair.

"Hey, Honey, I don't have any experience with Eyetalian haircuts. Can you tell me exactly what to do?"

"Of course. Piece of cake for you, Callie." I pulled out a couple of sketches I had drawn showing how I cut Art's hair, and handed them over.

"I see," was Callie's comment, "Kinda different from the usual Tennessee Marine skin-head type!" We both laughed. "Sure, I'll cut his hair. Bring him over. Hey, is he one of those dream-boat type Eyetalians, with bedroom eyes like the ones in the movies?"

I considered Callie's joking question a moment, thinking

of Giovanni. 'You know, Callie, I'm going to let you figure that out and you can tell me the next time we talk." Callie was a statuesque former fashion model, nearly six feet tall, and Giovanni might just come up to her navel.

I turned back just before I left and added, "Oh, and Callie, Giovanni might prefer to call you a barber. Or you might tell him that's what you are. I don't know how the idea of his going to a woman's hairdresser would go down too well with him."

It was about two months later when the Beladinos came to dinner again, Giovanni, his pretty wife Carla and their three small boys. As they walked in, I noticed Giovanni glance in the mirror on the wall, and smooth his perfect Italian haircut down. As he walked past me he whispered, "Meesus Opton, I am so happy with that barber you find for me. Nowhere in Roma ees there a beautiful blond barber like her!"

Two Girls Hanging Out

There comes a time in most families, when the children ask for a kitten. Becky was 7, Melissa was 5 and Brad was 3 when the three of them started begging us to get a kitten. The timing of their request may have had something to do with the fact that our friends, the Alberts, had just told us about their new litter of black kittens. When Art heard this, he flatly said, "No! No kittens!"

I didn't worry about his anti-feline prejudices. He had never been around cats when he was growing up. His "No kittens" stance was nothing more than the normal reaction of many people who had never lived with a cat. Once we had a cat, Art would soon be completely won over by its feline charm. Cats are smarter than humans, and are skilled at playing hard to get, which is one of the more successful of the arts of flirtation, as all women and cats know.

As soon as the Alberts' kittens had their eyes open, we went over to see them. There were four beautiful tiny black fur-balls, and our children were enchanted. "Puleese, Mommie, puleese, Mommie. Make Daddy say "Yes!"

As it turned out, sheer numbers finally defeated Art. Four pro-cats against one anti-cat are tough odds to beat.

A couple of months later, we drove over to pick out our kitten. Penny met us at the door in tears. One of her kids had slammed the door on the tail of the prettiest kitten, cutting the tail halfway off. It was a messy, bloody sight. "I'm so upset, that poor little kitty has been in such pain. And now, nobody will want her."

"Don't worry, Penny" I smiled to reassure her. "Wait five minutes. That will be the first kitten adopted." I knew my three kids would feel so sorry for that injured kitten, she would be the only one they would want.

"Mommie," I was tugged aside by my three teary-eyed children, "This poor little kitty needs lots of love, now, Mommie," Becky said. "She needs to come live with us." Melissa and Brad nodded in agreement.

"Wonderful!" Even though I had expected them to choose this little maimed kitten, I still felt touched by my children's compassion. "You can talk about a name for her on the way home."

Soon our newly named Teeo, was fixed up with a box on the back porch, sheltered from the wind and rain. She stayed in the yard most of the time, and early in the morning there was always a furry little black face at the door to greet us.

Then, one cold rainy morning, there was no kitten waiting at the door. Worried, I went out in the yard and called and called, but Teeo didn't come. Then, about an hour later, two young boys knocked on the door, and said they had found a kitten lying in the rain filled gutter, badly injured. They knew it was our kitten. We were horrified to see our poor little Teeo soaking wet and half frozen, bleeding from bites all over her body. The boys had chased two dogs away from her.

We raced to the vet with her, expecting her to die any moment. Dr. Benson cleaned her up, sewed up the worst injuries, and told me to care for her by holding warm compresses to her injuries every couple of hours during the day and in the evening. Despite my care, Teeo's wounds were soon infected, and it became a marathon nursing experience, caring for her for the next few weeks. She must have been in terrible pain each time I had to hold warm, moist compresses against her wounds, but she never cried, nor tried to bite me. Then slowly her wounds subsided and began to heal, although she was left with lumps all over her body. We learned that cats' wounds heal quickly, but bacteria is often sealed into the wounds where it festers and causes abscesses, as Teeo's wounds had. Then, if the abscesses don't drain completely, they often become walled off, and the cat is left with lumps of scar tissue at the site of each wound or, in Teeo's case, at the site of each dog bite.

Afterwards, our poor little kitty was a homely, lumpy little black furry creature, with just half a tail hanging down. But never in my life have I known a sweeter, gentler cat. Somehow, she seemed to understand that we would take care of her, as I had, after the dogs attacked her. We always believed that her experience of being cared for day after day made her a totally trusting little cat. She learned to patiently accept whatever had to be done for her. We could pick her up, or even turn her upside down, and she never protested.

Teeo became an important part of our lives. And she used all her charms to make Art love her, as I knew she would. He even went so far as to suggest that we let her have a litter of kittens for the kids. We hoped they might have a chance to see Teeo giving birth. In due time, Teeo became pregnant, and, fingers crossed, we hoped the father was a handsome big Siamese cat hanging around the house.

Then Art was invited to an international scientific congress in England, the following summer and I planned to go with him. "Oh, no!" I said, "What if she has a litter she hasn't weaned when we have to leave?"

"No problem," was Art's answer. "We'll just ask one of the neighbors to take care of Teeo and the kittens until we return."

The kids were excited at the prospect of a litter of kittens, and they hovered over our little black expectant mother all during her pregnancy, patting her growing belly, and, putting their ears against her expanding waistline, as they tried to hear sounds of baby kittens. Our gentle little cat tolerated all of the loving attention, like any pregnant female, knowing that she deserved all good things in her delicate condition.

She gave birth to five beautiful little bundles of fur, two of them on our couch, with a cheering gallery of family members to encourage her. She was just as devoted a mother as we had expected.

The time of our trip to England was drawing near, so I began to canvass the neighborhood for someone to feed Teeo and her family while we were in England. Ironically, none of the cat lovers would help us, but one of the cat haters volunteered to feed Teeo while we were away. However, she would only care for Teeoh and not the kittens, and she insisted that we had to get rid of the kittens if we wanted her help. We agreed, and were able to find good homes for all the kittens.

We consulted our vet about giving Teeo's kittens away before they were weaned, and he gave her a shot to help dry up her milk. "However, she will need another couple of shots, and will be in pain from the pressure of the milk in her breasts. There is nothing we can do about that, except just wait until her milk dries up."

Teeo began to cry later that afternoon, so I picked her up for a cuddle. When I looked at her breasts, I saw they were engorged and leaking milk. She was clearly in pain, her plaintive little cries never stopping.

Suddenly, I remembered the terrible pain I suffered when I developed mastitis, a severe inflammation in my breasts, when Becky was born. At least in my case, I could nurse my baby and reduce some of the pressure. I knew just what our kitty was going through.

Looking at our poor little suffering kitty, I burst out, "Oh, you poor baby. I only had two breasts, and you have six of them, all hurting you at the same time. We girls have to hang together, and come up with a solution."

In the kitchen drawer, I located a plastic hospital straw and found that it fit perfectly over Teeo's nipples. I carried her out to the porch, and sat down in the big rocking chair

I had used to nurse my babies, and lay Teeo on her back on my lap. Then, moving slowly and gently, I carefully placed the straw over a nipple, and started sucking the milk, which I poured into a dish. As soon as I could see the tension of the breast ease up noticeably, I moved to the next breast, re-aligned the straw, and continued sucking. I was careful not to empty Teeo's breasts, as that would have stimulated more milk. I just wanted to ease the pressure so that she wouldn't suffer any more pain, while we waited for her milk to dry up. As soon as I sucked on the last breast, easing the pressure and stopping her pain, our little kitty stopped crying, and began to purr.

For the next several days, Teeo and I continued our regimen, she lying on my lap, belly up, while I sucked just enough milk from her breasts so she had no more pain.

The following week, when we returned to Dr. Benson's for another shot of drying medicine for Teeo, he took a close look at her breasts and said, "I've never seen a cat dry up this fast with only one shot of the medication. Why this is amazing. She doesn't seem to be in any pain at all. I don't think she needs a second shot to dry her any further." He looked puzzled.

"Well, now I'll tell you what she and I have been doing," I smiled at him.

When I described the routine that Teeo and I had developed, Dr. Benson burst into laughter. "My God!" he said, "This is the first time I ever had a pet owner actually nurse from one of our feline mothers! If I were your husband, I wouldn't kiss you for six months!"

Driving home, I decided that our female cat and I had more in common than we did with the average human male. Hanging out with Teeo and understanding what she was going through, gave me something to really think about. . .

Feathers and Fur

Caterina stopped by one day in mid-February to tell me she was taking her children back to Italy for a visit with her family. It had been several years since she had been home.

"Catti, that's wonderful! Your family must be dancing for joy! When are you leaving?"

"We leave the end of May and come back the end of July. I have a big favor to ask you. Will you take care of Debbie's new parakeet while we are away?"

I gulped. The thought of having to look at that tiny jail with that small jailbird in my house for two and a half months was depressing. I hate the idea of being a warden for any bird or animal in a cage. "Oh, Catti, please, let me keep the two dogs instead. I don't know anything about birds, but we'd all love to have your setters stay with us while you're gone." Our yard was fenced in for our spaniel, so it would be safe for the setters, as well.

"I am so sorry, Betsy, but we have arranged for somebody else to take care of the dogs. We should have asked you first. I just thought the bird would be so much easier."

"It's just that I have never taken care of a parakeet."

"Debbie knows that. But she really wants you to keep her bird. She is sure you will take good care of her beloved Tweety-Bird. This is the first time she has had her very own pet, and she trusts you with it."

I just stared at Catti. Debbie trusted me to care for her bird? Why me? I barely knew the child. However, Debbie knew that her mother and I were good friends, so perhaps Catti had led her to believe that I would be trustworthy and careful with her beloved Tweety-Bird.

My heart sank. I felt really stuck.

Even so, how could I refuse a good friend like Catti a favor like this? I knew how much she looked forward to visiting her family with her children.

So I put a big smile on my face and agreed. "Don't give it another thought, Catti, of course I'll keep Tweety-Bird for Debbie. But I need detailed instructions on what to do and what not to do."

"Oh, Debbie will be so happy! I told her you would take wonderful care of Tweety-Bird."

I went home, kicking myself for having gotten into something I knew I didn't want to do. Why did I give in when caring for the parakeet was something I dreaded so? Had I ever stood up for myself? I realized that my giving in was behavior so typical of women, but perhaps even more typical of me, with my "Obedient Army Brat" background. I had always done what other people asked me to do, not wanting to offend anyone. Of course I wanted to help Catti, but why could I not be honest with myself, and honest with friends about what I wanted to do or did not want to do?

May came and Caterina and Debbie brought Tweety-Bird over. Debbie carried the cage into the house. She looked around as any eleven year old would, to see whether our house would be suitable for her pet.

Then she turned back to thank me, "I know you'll take good care of my bird. He'll be happy at your house."

I gave Catti a hug, and they left. "Have a wonderful time," I called after them.

The routine of caring for the parakeet was easy. Each day I changed the paper on the floor of his cage, and made sure he had plenty of fresh water and birdseed. From time to time, I moved his cage near a sunny window, hoping to relieve what, to me, was a terrible limited life for a small bird.

Then, early one morning, at the end of the second week,

Art called me. "Betsy, come here. Something's wrong with the parakeet."

My heart sank, and I hurried out of the kitchen to the living room where the cage was hanging in a big window. To my horror, there was Tweety-Bird lying motionless on his back, his tiny feet curled over his still body. I opened the cage as fast as I could, hoping he would wake up when I touched him.

"Oh, Art! He isn't even warm to touch. Oh, no! What can we do? Poor Debbie trusted us with her pet. How can I tell them that we've let them down and killed her beloved bird?" I was on the verge of tears.

Art put his arms around me. "I am sure you did nothing wrong. You followed all the instructions carefully. Sometimes, animals just die, no matter how well they are cared for."

"They won't be home for another month and a half. I could get another parakeet like Tweety-Bird, but what if the second bird died before they returned? Maybe I really did do something terribly wrong." I moaned to Art.

"You can't let this get you down," Art said. "Let's just think of what to do now."

Suddenly, I looked at Art. "I know, I'll pop him into the freezer wrapped in plastic, then the week before they're due home, I'll take Tweety-Bird to the dime store and get one to match him. That way, nobody will ever know."

"Good idea," Art agreed.

Into the freezer went Tweety-Bird, carefully wrapped in his plastic funeral shroud. I took a deep breath and prayed it would all work out.

June came and about five days before Catti and her kids were due to return, I took the frozen body of Tweety-Bird out of the fridge. "I'll go with you, Mom," Melissa was stacking breakfast dishes into the dishwasher. "That way we can both look for a good match to Tweety-Bird and it will be much faster."

"Oh, that will be wonderful, Darling. I am sort of dreading this. What if someone who knows Cattie sees me holding a dead bird that we are trying to match to the ones for sale?"

"Don't worry, Mom. I can hold the dead bird so nobody will see him. It's going to all work out. You'll see." At thirteen, Melissa was a bulwark of confidence and reassurance whenever anything went wrong. Her giggle was infectious and we both began to laugh as we looked at the dead bird wrapped in plastic.

Still laughing I asked Melissa "Can you imagine what it would be like if we had taken care of Catti's dogs, and one of them had died. Can't you see us carrying the frozen corpse of a setter wrapped in plastic to a setter breeder to get a good match?"

The two of us nearly collapsed in laughter as we pictured having to deal with a dead dog in our freezer.

Melissa tucked Tweety-Bird into her lunch-box, dressed in his plastic shroud and we drove to the dime store in downtown Oak Ridge where they had a huge walk-in cage filled with noisy parakeets. I told the young salesman that we wanted to buy a parakeet, so he picked up a long handled net and started right into the cage.

"Please wait a minute," I called, "Let me show you what we want."

When he backed out of the cage and walked over, Melissa opened her lunch-box and surreptitiously pulled out the frozen body of Tweety-Bird, holding it so that no one except the young salesman could see the dead bird. "Here, look at this bird," she told the salesman.

"This is what we want," I told him. "We need an exact match."

The young salesman recoiled in horror. He didn't want to

touch the frozen little body. He gulped, "Where'd y'all git that there dead bird?"

"Never mind that, that's our problem. Now let's just find one exactly the same."

"Well now, Ma'am, that's gonna be kinda tricky," he started, just as I hurriedly interrupted.

"Wait! Look there on that branch! That looks just like this bird!"

He looked, "Oh yes, Ma'am. Now jes lemme catch 'em." He hurried back into the big cage, but just as he swung the net, all hundred or so birds started flying in a huge circle around the cage. He stood still, net ready. The three of us watched as all the birds landed on various perches. Then we stood there looking for a matching bird. Melissa reached in through the door holding the lunch-box with the frozen bird so the young salesman could look carefully at the color and pattern we needed. He still wouldn't touch Tweety-Bird's cold little body.

"Look there, Ma'am, there's two birds jes like your dead one. O.K. now, here goes."

Another swipe of his net sent all the birds flying around in another circle. He muttered under his breath. and I muttered under mine.

We waited for the birds to calm down again. Each time the flock of parakeets alighted, they settled on different perches, so it took time for the three of us to spot where the two matching birds were. Then the young man had to cautiously move around the cage, careful not to disturb the birds, slowly get into position, aim and swing his net, but each time the birds were too fast for him to catch the particular bird he aimed for. If I had just wanted a parakeet, any parakeet, the young man would have caught one with his first swing of the net. But trying to see where a particular bird was perched, one close to the exact color and pattern of Tweety-

Bird, then watching carefully to single him out as he joined the rest of the flock flying in circles, and then swinging the net to catch him: that was a different story. I was beginning to realize what a demanding request I had made.

Forty minutes had gone by. The young man kept swinging his net, without success.

"Maybe we should just quit. You're getting tired. Come on out and sit down while we talk this over."

He came out, closed the door of the birdcage and sat down with us.

"Ma'am, would you mind explainin' why it has to match that there dead bird you got?"

So I told him about Debbie and my caring for her bird while she was away. I was on the verge of tears, as I explained how terrible I felt when I found the dead bird.

By then, the young bird-catcher was on a first name basis with Melissa and me.

"Look here, Betsy, and Melissa, we're not hardly done yet. I'll git a bird for y'all before you know it." Jake was determined that we were going to succeed. "I don't want to look back someday and say I jes quit, and let a little bitty bird win."

Jake went back into the cage, and again the hunt began. As he continued to swing at first one bird, then another, we became aware that a crowd had gathered around the big parakeet cage. At first, it was just the store clerks who weren't busy, then customers crowded around to watch. They were very quiet as they watched. Now and then someone would say, "Hey, that bird on the top branch, looks just like your dead one!" Then Jake would take a swing. This was repeated over and over, as Jake tried repeatedly to catch one of the two matching birds. He had some near catches, but each time the wily little parakeets would elude his net.

I glanced a my watch, and to my horror saw that we had been at it for nearly two hours. "Jake," I raised my voice,

"Time to call it a day."

Just then as Melissa and I turned to leave, there was a whoop from Jake, "Got him!"

Cheers broke out all over the store. Jake came out of the cage, perspiring but grinning like a Cheshire cat. "He's the perfect match. Look here, Betsy, see if he isn't. What do you think, Melissa?""

"Wow! You did it, you wonderful, patient man!" I threw my arms around Jake. All three of us were feeling so happy. We had the perfect bird for Debbie and a new buddy at the dime store.

When Caterina returned with the kids from her trip, she came and took Tweety-Bird, the Second, home to Debbie.

She called me the next day. "Betsy, you won't believe this. Debbie insists that that's not her bird. I told her that of course it's her bird, 'Why, Debbie, Mrs. Upton has taken good care of him for you.'"

I laughed off Debbie's insistence that that wasn't her bird. "Good grief," I thought, "Why would she doubt it? It looks exactly like Tweety-Bird the first, same colors, same patterns, same chirp."

It wasn't until two weeks later that I understood. I had gone to the vet to pick up Teeo, our black cat, whom I had left the day before to have her teeth cleaned under anesthesia. A young temporary assistant came out with a black cat in her arms, "Here's your cat."

"Wait a minute, that's not my cat!"

"Oh, sorry," she said and went back and brought out my cat. "You know, as far as I can see, all black cats look just the same. You could switch them around and never know the difference.

I was indignant, "Just a minute, what do you mean all black cats are the same? That's nonsense. Why, they all have different personalities..."

Suddenly I stopped, and in a flash I thought of Tweety-Bird and realized that I had always believed that all parakeets were the same, just different colored feathers…

Of course Debbie knew that wasn't her Tweety-Bird. She was never fooled. I was only fooling myself.

I never talked to Debbie about her bird after that. I let time go by without seeing her and telling her how sad I was when her bird died. Perhaps she would have understood my reasons for thinking that I could spare her grief by getting her a new bird that resembled her Tweety-Bird. Perhaps, also, she would have understood the anguish I felt when I found her little bird dead in the cage.

In the years since that spring, I have never come to terms with what I did, nor the way I tried to resolve the death of her bird by substituting a different bird. I have often wished I might have a chance to talk to Debbie, and apologize about my lie. I'd also like to know if Debbie came to love Tweety-Bird the Second.

Home Sweet Home

I was returning from a trip to a meeting in Atlantic City where Art had given a paper. He was going on to another conference, while I flew home to the family. The airport closest to Oak Ridge was in Knoxville, Tennessee. My flight home was delayed, but luckily there was always an airport limousine waiting to take passengers to Oak Ridge, no matter how late it was.

In addition to me, there were several visiting engineers who were on their way to a conference in Oak Ridge, as well as one other Oak Ridge resident. The latter was an older man who was a well-known physicist named Zeligmann. He had emigrated to the U.S. from Hungary and then was recruited to work in one of the major research laboratories in Oak Ridge. On the long drive to Oak Ridge from Knoxville, the five young engineers were a talkative group, enthusiastic about this first visit to the town, and eager to see what the lab and the research facilities were like. They plied me with questions about the interesting people they had been told lived there. I tried to emphasize the wide variety of people living and working in Oak Ridge, but I sensed that they considered most of the residents to be mad scientists.

When we arrived in Oak Ridge, the limousine driver began to drop off the first passengers at the east end of town. On this evening, the first passenger to be taken home was Dr. Zeligmann. He lived at 104 Dover Lane, he told the limousine driver, which was a short dead-end lane that ran just off Delaware Avenue.

The driver called back to Dr. Zeligmann, "Suh, Ah'm a new drivah, so Ah may need some directions."

"Ees next right driver," Zeligmann suddenly spoke up.

"No, Driver!" I burst out. "That's not Dover Lane, it's Disston." I had friends who lived there.

"Oh, you are right. Thenk you veddy much, thenk you veddy much," Dr. Zeligmann said to me.

As we approached the next street off to the left from Delaware, I saw Dr. Zeligmann lean forward, and tell the driver to turn at that corner.

Again, I stopped the driver, "No, no, Driver. Dover Lane is up at the top of the hill. I know which it is."

Again, I received gracious thanks from Dr. Zeligmann. "So kind. Thenk you veddy much, thenk you veddy much."

We drove past two more side streets, when Dr. Zeligmann again told the driver to turn at the next corner.

Again, I had to interrupt, "No, Driver. Dr. Zeligmann is mistaken. Dover Lane is farther up the hill."

"You'll jes lemme know, Ma'am?" the driver asked. "It's gitten late and I know ya'll must be real tard."

Looking in the rear view mirror, I could see the driver yawn.

"Of course," I reassured the driver. "Turn left at the second corner." I heard the driver let out a sigh.

"Which house, suh?" the driver asked Zeligmann.

"End of street," Zeligmann replied.

"Dr. Zeligmann," I interrupted, "that's not your house. That's where the Marshalls live."

"Oh, you are right. Thenk you veddy much."

"Well, now," said the driver, "Looks like to me that that there is your house, suh. 104 Dover Lane."

There were cars parked immediately in front of Dr. Zeligmann's house, so the limousine pulled over in front of his next-door neighbors' house. Dr. Zeligmann got out of the limousine, and started up the sidewalk to his neighbor's house.

The driver called out, "Suh, suh, that ain't your house.

Your house is next door." Then, leaning out the window of the shuttle, he added, "I reckon ya'll must be new in this heah neighborhood."

Dr. Zeligmann stopped, turned around and said, "Oh no, driver. Vee haf lif here now twenty-von years."

As the limousine drove away, one of the visiting engineers turned to me and said, "Whew! I hope there aren't many more like him here."

I just laughed and told the truth: "Hundreds!"

Bible Belt

When we moved to Oak Ridge, I didn't pay much attention to the fact that we were in the Bible Belt. All I had heard about the Bible Belt was that, at the end of the 18th Century, before roads had been built, evangelical preachers traveled on horseback from one remote Christian community to the next, where they held revival and camp meetings, preaching hell-fire and damnation. Thus, evangelical fundamentalist Christianity became the dominant way of life in East Tennessee.

However, Oak Ridge was very different from the rest of Tennessee. Art's fellow Biology Division scientists had moved to Oak Ridge from many parts of the US, as well as other countries. They specialized in a variety of scientific studies such as plant physiology, genetics, or pathology, which was Art's field.

There was still a fence around the entire town, with guards at each entrance. We felt very separated from the rest of Tennessee. It was hard to imagine that fundamentalist Christianity would ever touch our lives, as our community was made up of so many families of different religious and cultural backgrounds.

In the beginning, my friendships developed from contacts with other young mothers. We talked about our children, or schools or what was going on in town or parties. The subject of religion seldom came up. Once in a while, friends would invite us to visit their church, knowing that Art and I were not affiliated with any church in town. We never accepted invitations to go to church, and both of us enjoyed the community and the friends we made. For three or four years, Art and I enjoyed the open atmosphere of Oak

Ridge, and the apparent acceptance of different religious and cultural traditions.

Then the Bible Belt buckle smacked me right in the face.

One of my closest friends was a charming North Carolina woman, whose husband was director of one of the big divisions at the Laboratory. They had invited us to join one of the many dance clubs that had started in town, so we saw them often. As the years went by, I cherished my friendship with Carolyn, and we got together nearly every week.

One day, she telephoned, "Betsy, ah want you to help me. I'm goin' to start a protest about the swimmin' pool. It shouldn't be open on Sunday mornin'. I have a list of people who want to help. We need to demand that it be closed durin' church services."

I was stunned, and tried to think of how to reply. Finally I said, "But Carolyn, that's a public pool. Maybe Christians won't swim on Sunday, but there are many people in town who aren't Christians. You know that. There are Jews, Muslims and others, who don't go to church. For that matter, what about the Seventh Day Adventists? They're Christians, but they don't hold their services on Sunday."

She became furious. "Well, I doan care! Ever'body ought to be in church on Sunday mornin'!"

Soothingly I said, "Oh, Carolyn, you don't mean that. You and Richard have Jewish friends. You don't want to keep them from swimming if they want to."

"If you doan agree with me you cain't be mah friend!" The phone slammed down in my ear.

That was the end of our friendship. She would have nothing to do with a sinner like me, standing up for those non-Christians, who should be in church with the true believers.

Then I discovered the Bible Belt in the schools.

When our younger daughter, Melissa, started first grade,

she was already an avid reader. For the first couple of months of school, her favorite book was one about different religions. She brought it home from the school library, and the whole family talked about it at dinner.

Soon afterwards, I had a phone call from Melissa's teacher, asking me to come in for a conference. Mrs. Allen was warm and loving, a truly gifted teacher.

When I went in to meet her, she sounded worried, "Mrs. Upton, Melissa's a real joy to teach. She is so eager to explore the world of ideas. However, I must tell you that I worry about her. The other day she told the class that Jesus and those others didn't interest her. Buddha was the one for her. Oh, Mrs. Upton, we can't leave these choices to her."

"Mrs. Allen, you mustn't worry. My husband and I believe in firm spiritual guidance for our children. We are sure that Melissa's interest in Buddha is just a passing fancy."

"You don't know how much I appreciate your coming in, Mrs. Upton. I feel so much better now."

Then, when our older daughter, Becky, was in the sixth grade, she was taught by Mr. Owens, a new young teacher. He began a science unit on anthropology and archaeology, but knowing that Tennessee law forbade him to teach evolution, he assigned different topics for the students to write about. Becky was asked to give a report on Darwin's Theory of Evolution.

That evening and many following evenings, our telephone rang non-stop with hate calls. One man sounded threatening, calling us Satan-inspired sinners.

The following day, young Mr. Owens called me to apologize. He had no idea that his assignment for Becky would expose us to so much anger from the fundamentalists in town.

Then, the following year Becky started seventh grade. The first week, she came home, very upset. "Mom, every

Monday Mrs. Gresky asks everyone in social studies class if they went to church on Sunday. Everybody has to raise their hands if they did. Then, she asks anyone who didn't go, to raise their hands. She makes those kids sit on the floor in the hall, wearing a sign around their neck saying, "I am a sinner. I did not go to church on Sunday." They miss half the class. Mom, it's awful. It's not fair!"

I was outraged. The following day I went to see the principal of the junior high. As I began to tell him what Mrs. Gresky was doing to the non-Christian students on Mondays, he quickly interrupted.

"Now, Mrs. Upton. Mrs. Gresky is one of air best teachers, and a real fine Christian lady. I just cain't believe that she would be so un-Christian to her students. Jest go on home and tell your little girl to stop makin' up stories!"

Angrily I burst out, "Mr. Willard, next Monday I will be here, and you and I will go to Mrs. Gresky's room together. We'll see whether my daughter is making up stories."

The following week I returned to the principal's office. He and I walked down the hall to Mrs. Gresky's room, and when he saw the children sitting on the floor in the hall, he became quite upset. Then he turned and made an embarrassed apology to me. After that, Becky reported that Mrs. Gresky never asked that question again and nobody ever had to sit in the hall.

Then, in May, my hope that tolerance still existed was restored.

I was shopping at Penney's, where I ran into my friend Anne, looking glum. When I asked what was wrong she told me that her son Arnold was going to celebrate his bar mitzvah the following spring.

"Why, that's wonderful!" I answered.

"Well, it would be wonderful, only we have a new rabbi. Our reform rabbi left, but the new one is conservative. Any food taken into the Temple must be Kosher." She looked anguished. "I don't know a thing about Kosher cooking! What will I do?"

I wasn't surprised that Anne knew nothing about Kosher cooking. She was a classics scholar who taught Greek and Latin at the University of Tennessee in nearby Knoxville. There wasn't any kind of cooking that interested Anne.

I thought about it for a couple of minutes, then said "Hey, Anne, here's what you'll do. Go ask the rabbi if a non-Jewish friend can cook for Arnold's bar mitzvah. I'll follow all the dietary laws. I'll buy new pots and pans, new mixer blades, new spoons, new platters, everything. I know about heating up the oven, to purify it before I bake anything. Then you can come and take stuff I cook and stick it into a freezer somewhere."

"Oh, Betsy! I can't let you do that! It will be so much work for you."

"Look, you know I love to cook, with all the visiting scientists we entertain. It will be fun."

Then I clinched the argument, "Besides, one of my kids will probably marry someone Jewish! I may need separate stuff when that day comes."

Anne called me that evening, "Wonderful news! Rabbi Benjamin says it will be all right for you to cook for Arnold's bar mitzvah. I told him you will follow all the rules."

The next morning another Jewish friend called. When I told her what I was going to do, she said, "Hey, how silly to buy all that separate equipment. Who would ever know?"

"I would," I said, realizing that Rabbi Benjamin had decided to trust me to follow the rules for Kosher baking. I truly felt honored.

Next morning, I bought all the clean new kitchen equipment and dishes, then stopped at the grocery store for eggs, sugar, flour, and other ingredients I needed to start with. The following morning I began to bake. Every day I tried different recipes, old ones, new ones, borrowed ones, traditional ones and untried exotic ones from esoteric cookbooks: apple cake, banana-nut cake, blintzes, lemon tarts and hazelnut torte. I even baked my favorite Hungarian desert, Dobos Torte, but I realized that it was not designed to be cut into pieces and frozen, so we ate it.

The months passed, and Anne stopped by every few days to carry out the containers and packages of my Kosher baking. For me, those were memorable months of creative fun, with our house always smelling like a wonderful bakery. I never enjoyed myself more.

Finally the day came when Anne told me, "Enough already!" laughing as she said it. My life as a big production Kosher baker had come to an end.

Many years later, when I recounted my experience as a Kosher baker to Jewish friends in New York, they told me that no Conservative Rabbi would ever have given me, a non-Jew, permission to bake for Arnold's bar mitzvah. I must have been mistaken. He must have been a reform rabbi.

I didn't say anything, but I knew better. Then, as I thought back to my year as a Kosher baker, I wondered whether Rabbi Benjamin might have felt so repelled by the prejudice and narrow-mindedness he had encountered in the area, that he decided to be more accepting. I have always believed that he must have decided that his God probably wouldn't hold it against me if I weren't Jewish, so why should he?

I kept my Kosher kitchen equipment separate until the day our son, Brad, married Mindy, our beautiful Jewish daughter-in-law. However, I soon discovered that I no longer needed to continue to keep anything Kosher.

Mindy wasn't Jewish anymore. She was a Buddhist.

Cheese Soup

In 1951, when we moved to Oak Ridge, it was the era of the stay-at-home-mom.

For me, it was a wonderful life while our children were young. I loved spending time with my kids. Even so, much as I enjoyed our girls, and later our son, Brad, and being at home with them, whenever I thought about the future, when our children were older, I worried that I would find staying at home an empty existence. Housework bored me and I often felt envious of Art for having an interesting and absorbing job.

Oak Ridge was the quintessential one-company town. The Oak Ridge National Laboratory had established strict nepotism rules. Nobody was allowed to work at the Laboratory if they already had a family member working there. Aside from the Lab, the only possibilities for work were a few hamburger drive-ins, a couple of clothing stores and a cafeteria. I couldn't see any future career possibilities there.

So, for several years, I stayed home and enjoyed our children while they were young. Then one day, my friend Martine called asking me to help her teach a literacy class she was starting. "Betsy, I'm starting an exciting project. It's a reading class for adults, and I already have a group of women who are delighted that this will be available for them. Will you come to the class next week? I'd love to have you teach with me. You'd be really good with these students, building their confidence and making them feel comfortable while they try to master something as hard as reading."

"Wait a minute, Martine. Your reading class is a great idea, but I have absolutely no experience as a teacher. I don't honestly know whether I'd be a help or a hindrance. Better get someone with experience."

"No, I want you. Please just give it a try, won't you? If you need to read about teaching techniques, I can lend you books I've used in the Special Ed class I used to take at the University. I started this class this past Wednesday and I've begun to kind of arrange the way we'll work, so come this week and just look in."

I was impressed by Martine's basic organization when I arrived at the class two nights later. Small groups of students sat, working quietly with each other. Some were reading, while their companions listened attentively. Some followed along with their fingers, pointing to each word in their own books, while others repeated the words to themselves, their lips moving silently. In several small groups, I noticed pairs of students who were assigned to work with each other. I walked around the classroom, introducing myself. The students were pleased to show me the books and workbooks that Martine had given them the week before.

Martine's students were all women, a racially mixed group, mostly African American and Caucasian, although I saw one Asian woman sitting in the back of the room. They ranged in age from their early twenties to a white-haired African-American woman in her late seventies. Martine had told me that she had joined the class because she wanted to be able to read her Bible before she died.

Before the class, Martine also explained that there was a wide range of reading skills among the students. Some had had very little schooling, and were beginning readers. Others had gone to poor schools, where they had learned to read, but only at a low level. It soon became evident that all of them hoped that they would be able to get better jobs once they improved their reading and writing.

Martine called me over to meet a young woman who had just walked into class. At first glance, she didn't appear to be more than sixteen or seventeen, dressed in a faded cotton dress that hung on her thin frame, holding a worn sweater wrapped tightly around her fragile body. She glanced nervously around the room.

"Betsy, this is Addie," Martine smiled. "Addie wants to learn to read menus so she can work in a restaurant. She needs tutorial help more than a group situation. Will you help her?" Martine handed me a stack of menus.

My heart sank. What was I doing there? I realized that I was about to be trapped by Martine into taking on a project in the form of a pitiful, skinny little mountain girl who needed help. "Martine," I called, "Addie needs someone with experience…"

"You'll pick it up quickly," Martine smiled over her shoulder as she walked away to a group of women around a table.

I smiled at Addie, "All right, let's get started." I pulled out several menus from a restaurant in a nearby town and asked her to read.

Hesitantly, her hands shaking as she held the menu, she began to slowly read the words on the menu, her finger pointing to each word she read. Each time she came to an unfamiliar word, she stopped and looked up at me, her big gray eyes fixed fearfully on my face, waiting for my reaction. I looked down at the wan little face of that thin, undernourished Tennessee mountain girl, and grinned at her. When she grinned back, it was as though the sun had burst through the clouds. Suddenly, I saw a pretty girl with a pert nose, a beautiful mouth and a dimple in her left cheek when she smiled. Straight blond hair brushed back for her forehead emphasized the delicate bone structure of her face.

At our first session together, I realized that my own hands were shaking as I gripped a copy of the menu Addie was reading. I burst out laughing, startling my nervous young student. "Just look here at my hands shaking, Addie! Looks like I'm more nervous than you, and I'm supposed to be the teacher. I guess we'll just have to learn together, what do you say?"

That broke the tension, and Addie giggled as she looked back at me. From that moment on, the two of us began to work as a team. Gradually she learned to sound out unfamiliar words, and as time went on, she seldom made a mistake. I often pretended to be the client ordering a meal, and she had to write the items down on a pad. Sometimes she would read off the specials of the day.

I learned that she had grown up in the Cumberland Mountains with five siblings. Addie loved school, and each fall, she started school with great hopes of staying all winter. Then, each year, when cold weather came, the children had to stay home because the parents could not afford to buy them shoes to wear. Addie practiced at home as much as she could, and beyond menus, now was determined to really learn to read well.

Both Martine and I were delighted to see the progress this determined young woman was making. I was also secretly pleased with what I was learning about teaching, working with Addie and, later, in the evening, reading Martine's books on education. Addie had mastered the vocabulary on the menus she had started on, and she was beginning to read some of the books the class provided.

One day, after class, I gave her some menus from a couple of New York restaurants and urged her to take them home for practice.

The following class period, I was met by a sobbing Addie. "Oh, Miss Betsy, hit ain't a bit a use my tryin' to larn to read. I thought I was larnin' good, and now I know I was'n."

I wrapped my arms around her and held her until she stopped sobbing. "Now, let's see why you think you aren't learning."

She pulled away from me, reached into her bag and pulled out a menu. Pointing to the selection of soups, Addie started to cry again, "Oh, Ma'am, I cain't figger out what this here soup name is. It looks like 'cheese' soup to me, but I know I'm jest readin' it wrong. There ain't no such thing as cheese soup. Now I know that I'll never larn to read!" She started to cry again.

"Now, wait a minute, darlin'." I said, "You did not make a mistake. That does say 'cheese soup' and that restaurant does have 'cheese soup' on their menu. You are right, you read it perfectly."

She looked at me, a joyful smile spreading across her face. "I done read it right?"

"Yes, you did. Now, all you have to do is sound out the words, and learn to trust yourself."

The following week, I handed Addie the menu from a French restaurant , and folding my arms, I stood in front of her with a smile. "O.K., go on and read it…"

She looked at me, "Oh, you're tryin' to trick me, I jest know you now. Oh no!" she burst out laughing as she read over the menu, "You ain't gonna tell me folks really eats snails and frogs legs?"

I nodded and smiled, "You see, you really can read, can't you?"

It was about two months later that Addie came in and proudly told the class that she had been hired to work as a waitress in a big café in Harriman, a town about an hour's drive from Oak Ridge.

Martine and I kept hoping that Addie would come in to visit the class sometime. We were anxious to know how she was getting along. When spring came, I suggested to Art that we drive to Harriman and buy some plants at the big nursery there. "I'd like to have lunch at Addie's café and see how she's doing." He agreed, so we loaded the kids into the car one weekend, and headed for Harriman.

After we bought some flats of flowers, and two small Chinese Holly shrubs, we drove to the big café where Addie had been hired.

I asked the headwaiter if I could have Addie wait on our table, and I was shocked when he said that she wasn't working there anymore. I stood there, feeling sick to think that she had lost her wonderful job. The headwaiter seemed to notice my distress and asked me. "Is there something I can do, Ma'am?"

I told him how distressed I was about Addie, and he gently stopped me. "Oh, Ma'am, she worked jest fine here, but left when she got a better job at the Harriman Inn. That's a new restaurant over on the other side of town. Y'all go on over there and have lunch, and Addie will be happy to see you."

When we drove to the Harriman Inn, Art and I and the kids went in ask for a table. The pretty blond hostess was taking another couple to a table. As she walked back towards us, I burst out, "Addie! You're the hostess here!"

"Why, Miss Betsy, I started out as a waitress here, and they said I was doin' real good in that job, but then the hostess moved away, and they offered me the hostess job. I love it, because I meet all the nice folks who come here to eat. And Miss Betsy, I'm engaged to be marrit. My boyfriend is the cook at the Harriman Café where I worked when I first came here. Miss Betsy, I jest want you to know, ever since I larned to read my life has jest turned out wonderful!"

Abracadabra!

Lisa asked if I'd like to ride over to Knoxville with her. She needed to stop at the University of Tennessee, as she was starting graduate classes that fall, beginning the course work for a Master's degree in Sociology. I was delighted to spend the day with her and visit the university. High spirited and full of fun, Lisa was always good company, and a delightful friend.

We had met in an Obedience Class for dogs. I had taken our Springer Spaniel puppy to train and I was amused by the striking red-haired woman whose Irish Setter had the same glowing hair color. As we left after that first training session, she muttered to me, "My husband needs this as much as our dog does!" We stood there laughing together. Usually vivacious, today Lisa seemed unusually subdued, her blue eyes troubled, as I got into her car.

On the drive over to Knoxville, Lisa confided to me that she was worried because her scores on the Graduate Record Exam were very uneven. Although she had scored at the extreme top of the chart on verbal skills, her math score was about as low as it could go. "Betsy, any lower, and my math scores would slide right off the the bottom of the page."

"Yes, but Lisa, you were accepted into the program. How much math do you actually need for Sociology?"

"It's statistics. I don't know how I'm going to handle statistics, my math background is practically nonexistent."

I just laughed. "Haven't I ever told you that the only proof I have of my own superior intelligence is the fact that I managed to sneak through Michigan without taking a single math or science course?" She laughed with me. Lisa and I both went to the University of Michigan at the same time, although we didn't meet until years later in Oak Ridge.

Nevertheless, she told me that, despite her poor math score, she had had an encouraging interview with the chairman of the sociology department, and he had accepted her application.

"I think he saw how interested I am in the field, and he told me he was sure that I can do the work. As far as math goes, he suggested some tutoring to help me."

"Smart man! He knows you'll do well, and you will. I have no doubt about that. You're making a wise decision. There sure aren't any jobs in Oak Ridge, but this could open up a teaching job for you somewhere in the area. Who knows?"

After that day together, I didn't see Lisa again except when we ran into each other at the grocery store or the drug store. She seemed a bit tense, but that wasn't surprising, since she had a full schedule of classes plus her family to care for.

Then, about a month later she telephoned, "Oh, Betsy, I'm a wreck. I am going to flunk out of graduate school. And there's nothing I can do about it." She started to cry so I just stood there holding the phone and waited until she stopped sobbing.

Then I asked what made her think she was failing.

"We have our first statistics test next week and I can't possibly pass it. Statistics classes are just hideously difficult, and even with the extra math tutoring, I still find it hard to work out the problems."

"Lisa, stop, calm down." On a sudden whim, I asked, "Now, when is your test?"

"It's next Thursday morning."

"O.K., so it's next Thursday. But tell me exactly what time it's scheduled to begin, and exactly what time it will end."

"Oh, well, it starts at 10 and ends at 11. But I'll be dead by eleven."

"No you won't. Now, listen to me, you are going to ace

that class…"

Hysterical laughter interrupted me. "Oh, Betsy, please don't joke."

"No, Lisa, I am not joking. I am going to think 100's for you next Thursday, beginning on the dot of 10 o'clock and stopping at 11. You will get an A in that exam."

There was silence at Lisa's end. "You make me feel so much better. Thank you for your patience. But, really, I don't want you to waste the whole hour thinking of me."

"Just listen to me, I told you, I will definitely be thinking 100s, and you are going to ace the test. Just believe me."

The following Thursday, at nine-thirty I was the car with Cindy, our Springer puppy, taking her to the vet for shots, but I kept glancing at the clock on the dashboard. On the dot of 10AM I began to think 100's for Lisa. At 11 am, I put it all out of my mind.

The phone rang Monday afternoon. Lisa was manic with joy, "Betsy, you won't believe this! I got a hundred on the test! We just got our test papers back today! An A in statistics! I can't believe it."

"Well, of course you got an A. Didn't I tell you that you would ace it? I'm not surprised at all."

A couple of weeks later, Lisa called again, and somewhat hesitantly asked, "Betsy, I have a major test in another class coming up next Wednesday. Will you think 100's for me again?"

"Of course. Just give me the day and the hour, Lisa."

So, when she called me two days after that test, thrilled with her A, I was delighted but again not surprised. After that, each time Lisa had a quiz or a major exam she was worried about, she would call and I would think 100's for her. My only requirement was that I had to know the exact date and hour, so I could schedule it into my life.

The following year, Lisa was completing the coursework

for her Masters degree, and I continued our schedule of my thinking 100's for her. I heard by the grapevine, that the chairman of sociology had told a Spanish professor that he had never had such a brilliant student. I just smiled to myself.

That October, my sister Nan telephoned from Michigan. She had been taking classes in psychology at a nearby college. Then she confided, "Please don't tell anyone, Bets, I am thinking about applying for the masters' program at some of the colleges in the area. But I know I won't get in, so I don't want anyone but you to know about it."

"Don't be silly, of course you'll get in. Then whenever you have an exam that makes you nervous, I will think 100's for you." I explained how I had been doing this for my friend, Lisa.

Nan just laughed, "Good grief, does she really think you have anything to do with it?"

"Who knows, and who cares? As long as it gives her confidence, because you know as well as I do that all I am doing is giving her the extra shot of confidence she needs."

Nan said, "Well some people sure do believe in weird stuff…"

My sister was accepted for her psychology program as she had hoped, although she sounded very worried and doubtful that she would be up to the course work.

A month later, she called again, "Bets, I know this sounds silly, but I am really nervous about my first exam next week. Would you please think 100's for me?"

"Of course I will. Just tell me the day and hour. You are going to ace this test, believe me."

She did, and did it make a believer of her? Who knows and who cares? My sister, that doubter of my magical powers, continued to call before every exam she was worried about. She enjoyed her classes so much and did so well on her exams that I was as delighted as if I were her fairy godmother.

Meanwhile, Lisa was completing her M.A. that June. I was feeling sad as the semester came to the end, because she and her family were going to move to Philadelphia in August where her husband had accepted a job. I would miss her friendship, the fun of thinking 100's for her, and her joyful telephone calls after each exam to tell me her grade. She was thrilled with her 4.0 grade average, all A's. It had given her so much confidence that she planned to go on and get her PhD.

She called just after all her exams had ended, "You know, Betsy, I never believed in any kind of mysticism or hocus pocus stuff before last year, but I do now when I realize what your thinking 100's has done for me. You really must have some kind of magical powers!"

"Nonsense, Lisa. All I did was build up your confidence. You really didn't need help from me."

At the end of summer, I stopped at Lisa's to say good-bye. She had been accepted into the PhD. program at the University of Pennsylvania. I was thrilled for her, and told her I knew she would do well.

The fall went by. Then early in January, my doorbell rang. It was Lisa.

"Lisa!" I shouted, "What a wonderful surprise!" We flung our arms around each other, as we went inside to talk.

"Oh, Betsy, you don't know how I have missed you. I finished the semester at Penn, but I just couldn't go on there without you so I've transferred back to U.T. I know I can finish my doctorate with you thinking 100's for me."

"Wonderful! We'll be able to see each other once in a while. I have really missed you. So, remember, just call before your first test, and tell me what time it starts and what time it ends. You'll ace it…"

Mr. August and His Christmas Cheer

Art was halfway out the lake cottage door, about to get into the car to drive to work in Oak Ridge, when he paused, "By the way, why don't you stop at Mr. August's on your way to the store this morning, and see if he has any empty barrels we can buy. I noticed he has some stacked behind the house, alongside the driveway."

Art had designed and built a clever, floating dock we kept moored on the lake in front of the cottage. He had built it about five years earlier when we wanted a dock sufficiently far out from the shore where the lake would be deep enough for the kids to learn to dive. Empty barrels were held under the dock as the flotation device. Recently we had discovered that two of the barrels had rusted a bit and developed slow leaks. The dock now listed slightly to one side, like a drunken sailor on shore leave. We definitely needed new barrels under it to keep it afloat.

The August's house was nearby, about a mile and a half from our cottage on Eagle Point Drive. From the lake when we rowed past, it was an impressive home built of a lovely rose-colored brick surrounded be shrubbery and flowers, a much more beautiful house than the summer cottages that most of us had. We could see a large garden off to one side, extending beyond the house for about an acre and a half, but it was too far from the lake to see what was planted there.

I called to Brad, "It's time to hit the road and go grocery shopping." He made a face and I made one back at him. He was nine that summer, full of the dickens and full of fun. Becky and Melissa were both away at camp in Georgia, so Brad and I were spending the time alone doing whatever we wanted to do. Grocery shopping was one thing neither one of us ever wanted to do, but he perked up when I added that we were going to stop at the August's first and see about buying some barrels.

As we drove into the their drive, Mr. August came out to greet us. "Well, now, howdy folks. It's about time us neighbors got acquainted." He called through the open door to his wife, who came out to meet us.

"Paul, why don't you take them out to eat some of your nice grapes?" Mr. August answered his wife, "Why, Mother, that's jest exactly what I'm fixin' to do."

He led us out to a huge vineyard, and took us along the rows of grapes, handing big bunches of grapes to Brad and me, as he identified the varieties; "Now here's some nice Chardonnay grapes. Have a taste of them. This here grape is one of my favorite sweet grapes, Grenache..." Up and down the rows he led us, as Brad and I stuffed ourselves with the grapes he piled into our hands, identifying each in turn, "Merlot, Pinot Noir, Muscat, Sauvignon Blanc...Most of these here grapes I bought over in France years back."

Brad and I followed along as he described the qualities of each variety of grape, both of us trying to be polite and eat the grapes he was piling in our hands.

Finally, looking at my watch, I said, "We'd better be going now, Mr. August," I said. "We have to get to Rockwood to..."

He interrupted, "Why you folks cain't leave until I show you my winery. You've only seen the vineyard. C'mon now. It's just down these here stairs, down under my garage. Y'all got all day to git to the Quick Chek."

He led us down a flight of stairs, and I was astonished to see all his professional winemaking equipment. He had bought it in France, he told us. The large room had shelves all along three walls, with rows and rows of bottles of wine. He reached up and took two large glasses down from the shelf, and pulled a bottle down.

"I'm going to let y'all taste my nice Merlot..." He filled both glasses to the brim, about 8 ounces of wine in each one.

"Oh, no, Mr. August," I remonstrated. "I'd love just a taste, but Brad is only nine years old. He can't have any wine."

"Why, Miz Upton, my wine doesn't have hardly any alcohol. It won't hurt this boy a bit. Notice that nice sweet undertone? I like my wine sweet. Course, I never drink wine, being Babdis, you know." Mr. August took a small sip from his small glass. When I turned to look over at Brad, out of the corner of my eye, I saw our host quickly empty his glass.

So, holding that big glass of wine, I decided to be polite, drink it and then leave. But before I started to get up, Mr. August had filled up two more glasses and handed them to Brad and me. "Now, I want y'all to notice the full body of this here white wine. It's one of my favorites. But, of course, I only taste my wine. I don't ever drink this, bein' Babdis, you know."

"Mr. August, if you don't drink your wine, what do you do with it?" I asked.

"Why I give it to Father Tom, over to Harriman. He's the Episcopal priest over there, and he likes my wine for the Communion service, you know. Father Tom, he says he never had better Communion wine. He comes over and we have us a tastin' session all day sometimes. What I mean, is, Father Tom does the tastin' since of course I don't drink, bein Babdis. I like my wine sweet, but now, Father Tom, he likes the dry wines I make. Here, lemme give you a sip of this one."

Before I knew it, I had another full glass of wine in my hand. I couldn't see Brad too clearly, it seemed sort of dark and misty where he sat, but I noticed that he had a glass in each hand.

"Mr. August, please don't give my boy any more wine. He's too young...."

"Jest don't you worry your pretty head, now, li'l Mother.

106

There's not hardly any alcohol in my wine. You kin ask Father Tom about that."

When I looked at my watch next, I thought it said eleven o'clock, but I knew that must be wrong since we had arrived around nine. I stood up, holding on to the back of the chair, "Mr. August, we've had a lovely morning, but now we must leave. Thank you so much for showing us your wonderful winery." I set down my empty glass, reached out and took both glasses that Brad was holding, and turned and slowly climbed the stairs, with Brad following, both of us clutching the railing, and putting each foot carefully on the next step. Mr. August came upstairs to see us off.

We talked briefly about the barrels we wanted to buy, and he agreed to help Art move them to our place on the weekend.

Then I added, "Your wines are dishush, I mean delicious. And they really don't have mush alcohol?"

"Why, Miz Upton, you couldn't hardly taste any alcohol, now could you? Well now, I'll tell you something, jes' between you and me, there's times when I almost wish't I was Episcopalian, instead of Babdis. But that's only the times when I have a new wine, one that Father Tom tells me is real special, because, of course, I cain't drink it, being Babdis, an all."

Brad and I got into the car, and drove off. How we made it to the Quick Chek, I'll never know. Why we went, well, that I do know. Mr. August's wine "didn't have hardly any alcohol in it" he told me, so I just decided to believe him and get the shopping over with while I felt so good.

Brad and I sailed through the normally boring grocery shopping. I remember we laughed a lot, and, then, as we loaded our groceries into the car and started home, Brad looked up at me and said, "Gee, Maw, grocery shopping sure was a lot more fun today."

Boating

When we bought our Tennessee cottage on Watts Bar Lake in the mid-fifties, the former owners left us a small wooden fishing boat. It was an extremely safe boat for our kids, with a high bow and unusually high gunwales. Art put a small outboard motor on it, which enabled us to take the whole family for rides, although most of the time we used it as a rowboat or for fishing close to shore. By a unanimous family vote, we painted it bright green and added two almond-shaped eyes to the bow, giving it the look of a wise and benevolent Asian deity.

As time went by and our children became good swimmers, we began to consider getting some sort of small sailboat. As a boy on Lake Michigan, Art had enjoyed sailing his family's sail canoe. In recent years Art's father, Uppie, had bought a larger sailboat for Art's younger brothers to enjoy, a size and category called a Lightning. We knew that the family wasn't sailing the Lightning much any more at Lake Michigan, and Art and I talked about buying it from his dad. However, we were reluctant to ask about it, for fear Uppie would think we were asking him to give us the Lightning, and might not realize that we expected to pay him for it.

Finally, we decided to buy a small sail boat called a Sunfish, which turned out to be great for hot summer days in Tennessee. It was perfect bathing suit sailing, as the flat deck was just a few inches above the level of the surface of the lake. Anytime we got too hot, we could stop, and one of us could dive over the side to swim and cool off.

It wasn't long before our Springer Spaniel discovered the pleasure of sailing with us on the Sunfish. Like all Spaniels, Cindy loved the water and swam often. So anytime she saw us getting ready to launch the Sunfish from our floating dock, she went racing down to the dock, her long Spaniel ears flying in the breeze, and was usually the first one on the Sunfish deck. She also paid close attention and learned nautical commands, so whenever the captain called out "Coming About! Hard to lee…" it was amusing to see our dog duck her head to avoid being hit by the boom, as the boat came about and changed directions.

The next time Art's parents came south to visit us, we took them down to see our cottage, and the first thing Uppie said, when he looked at the broad expanse of Watts Bar Lake, was, "I wish I had known you live on such a big lake. I just sold the Lightning this summer, and it would have been perfect for you on this lake."

Then, to Art's dismay, Uppie insisted that he would send down the big Chris-Craft inboard that nobody used anymore.

"Now look at the mess we're in," Art muttered to me, "What the devil will we do with a boat like that?" He tried to talk his dad into keeping the boat for the family to enjoy on Lake Michigan, but Uppie insisted that it was the perfect boat for us to have. He would have it put on a trailer and delivered to us as soon as he went home.

Art and I began to explore where to buy a boat house, where to keep the boat moored during the summer months, and what to do with it in the winter. The speedboats that our neighbors owned were new, lightweight fiberglass models, easily moored next to a small dock, as well as nearly no-maintenance. Both of us remembered Uppie's big Chris-Craft as an old-fashioned in-board speedboat, with beautifully maintained mahogany decks, and carefully matched fittings. Each winter it had been lifted out of the water and stored in dry-dock, and each spring it was carefully refurbished before being put back into the water. Where would that be possible in East Tennessee, where we lived?

However, before the boat was delivered to us, things began to fall into place. We located a boathouse, one that we could moor in the cove next to our cottage. It was pretty ugly, made of corrugated tin, rusting in places. However, once it had a new coat of green paint, to help it blend in with the bushes growing around the cove, it was not too obtrusive.

The day the boat arrived, Art and I must have looked like two spoiled second-graders, sulky, peeved and actually annoyed to be the recipients of such a princely gift. And princely it was. As soon as it was launched, both of us began to see that it would be a great boat for it the family. It was extremely sea-worthy, large enough to hold five to seven people comfortably, yet still easy to maneuver and to moor to our floating dock. In addition, and perhaps more importantly to our kids, it was a high-speed boat, perfect for water skiing, which we were all eager to learn.

The following weekend, Art arrived home at the cottage with two pairs of water skis, and a couple of life belts of different sizes.

"O.K. Who's going to be first?" was his question. Four pairs of eyes looked warily at those skis, the three kids' and mine, trying to decide.

By Monday morning, when Art left to drive back to work, all five of us had water skied, and our attitude toward that big Chris-Craft underwent a complete change. We now adored it!

It didn't take long to discover how much fun the speedboat added to all of the picnics we had during the summer. Many of our guests skied for the first time behind our boat, and others advanced to slalom skiing, using a single ski, which requires more skill in balancing. Perhaps the most fun were the times when we were able to teach timid beginners, and see the confidence build up as they learned.

As fall approached that summer, Art found out that the

speed boat could be stored in dry-dock at a marina in Kingston, a town located on the shore of Watts Bar up the river from our cottage.

Art's plan was to run the boat up to Kingston, to the dry-dock there early in the fall. We all wanted to make the trip with him, to see what the lake was like along the way. Other friends from Oak Ridge had cottages in different areas of Watts Bar Lake, so it would be a scenic trip. However, Art's travel schedule kept him so busy that it wasn't until just after Christmas that he had time to run the Chris-Craft up to Kingston.

When the weekend came for Art to make the trip, the weather was bitterly cold, so he insisted on making the trip to Kingston alone, promising the kids that we could all make the return trip together in the spring. I dropped him off at the small marina where the boat was temporarily moored that fall, and then the kids and I planned to drive to the big marina in the afternoon, where we would pick him up.

The morning Art decided to move the boat was a frigid winter day, with a gusty wind rippling the surface of the water. He left our boat dock early in the morning, heading out into the windy channel, up-river to Kingston.

The channel is clearly marked with buoys all the way, as there is a fair amount of river traffic heading up-river to Kingston. Art was careful to note the markers, and in many places, he could see that the river was dangerously shallow just beyond some of the buoys.

It was a long run from our part of Watts Bar Lake, and around noon it became colder as the sun went behind the clouds. Art calculated that he had another hour and a half before he would reach the Kingston marina. He was cruising along in an area where the navigable channel of the river was fairly narrow, yet the lake there was very wide. Art leaned over and looked carefully at the water, calculating the depth of the water within the safely marked river channel. It appeared to be deep water all along the channel marked with buoys.

This area of Watts Bar Lake wasn't heavily settled. He could see a few summer cottages built along one side of the river, with boat docks in front of several of them. Most of them were closed up, now that summer was over.

The trip was becoming tedious, and he was beginning to feel the cold seeping through the jacket he was wearing. Again, he leaned over the side of the boat, trying to determine the depth of the water. It looked very deep both inside the channel as well as the water 50 to 60 feet outside the buoys. Art decided that it should be safe to leave the marked channel and take a shortcut across the wide strip of open water, thereby cutting down the time of his trip.

Wham! The boat ran violently aground, nearly throwing Art overboard, as he peered into the water. Grabbing the wheel, he reversed the motion of the boat, trying to back off the sandbar. Nothing moved. He was definitely aground, and not likely to be able to move the boat off the sandbar without help.

Art tried signaling to the closest houses along the shore, yelling, whistling and waving his hands, hoping someone would see him. It was hopeless. He realized that he was going to have to push the boat off the sandbar himself, and he must do it soon, as the weather was getting colder and it would start getting dark soon. The only solution he could see was to strip off his clothes, get into the water and push the boat free. He hoped he could push it free by himself, and not discover that it was too firmly embedded in the sandbar.

He stood up in the boat, and began taking off his clothes, his heavy jacket and pants, flannel shirt, work boots and socks. Finally, he took off his undershirt, and finally just as he was taking off his underpants he heard a voice shouting,

"Wait! Help is coming!" Art looked towards shore and saw a couple waving from their dock, shouting to him.

Quickly, he put his clothes back on and waited for help. Soon he saw a small runabout putting out from shore, with two men sitting in it.

As they came alongside, one of them said, "Here, we'll get you free in no time."

"I'm sorry to be such a bother," Art apologized.

"Happens all the time," the younger man laughed. "Everybody thinks he can cut across that stretch of water and save time. We would have been here sooner, but our 11-year-old Patty was enjoying the show so much, she didn't mention you being in trouble. She usually calls the minute she sees a boat run aground, but this is the first time she has watched someone do a strip-tease in order to get in the water and shove his boat off himself. She wasn't about to stop the show before it got interesting!"

Every year after that, Art took the boat up river to Kingston early in the fall, and he usually invited a man to go along with him just in case they needed more muscle power to shove the boat off another sandbar. My own opinion was that Art would rather have someone else do a striptease if the boat ran aground again. He had already performed once for Patty. He didn't plan to star in another peepshow, ever again.

A Stitch in Time . . .

The phone rang. It was Robin, my neighbor Paula's youngest daughter. "Bets, may I come over and talk to you, as soon as possible?" She sounded upset.

"Of course, Sweetie. Come right now."

A few minutes later she walked in, a troubled look on her pixie face. Her mop of curls was tousled as she nervously ran her fingers through it. Robin's junior year at Duke University was over, so she was home for the summer waiting on tables at a local restaurant.

"Steven and I are getting married next June, after I graduate," she said, as we walked out to sit on the porch.

I threw my arms around her, "That's wonderful!" I added, "He's a grand boy and you two are perfect together. So what's bothering you?"

She made a comically woeful face, "I need your help, Bets. I am really desperate! Mother is determined to make my wedding dress, but you know Mother. She'll be sewing it up as I walk down the aisle! Please, you must talk her out of it. You are the only one who can do it."

I saw Robin's point immediately. Any dress Paula made would be a work of art, but she was not noted for her organizational skills.

Paula and I had always been friendly neighbors, but over the past year we had become close friends, driving to Knoxville together to take a class in tailoring. Most of the class had made women's suits, with a jacket and skirt. But Paula had chosen to make a jacket for her husband, instead. The class began in January and ended in May, but it was now mid-July and she had not finished the jacket.

I looked at Robin. When she saw my look of understanding, the tension drained out of her face. Grinning, she jumped up, clutched the front of her blouse, as if she were holding it together, and humming the wedding march, she staggered around. We both burst out laughing at her clowning.

"I'll do my best to talk her out of this project," I promised. "But you know your mother, she has strong opinions about things."

"Yes, I know, and we both know what a perfectionist she is about sewing. It takes her forever to finish anything, even when she is excited about it. You must, you must stop her from doing this!"

I hugged Robin, a sinking feeling in my heart, as I smiled at my young friend, "I'll try to talk her into buying you a beautiful dress."

The following day, I called Paula and invited her to come for lunch. Over shrimp salad and iced tea, I brought up the subject of Robin's wedding, "We are delighted at Robin's wonderful news. Steven is a fine young man, and they'll be a perfect couple."

"Yes, isn't it grand?" Paula responded. "Harry and I are so happy. We have been hoping that they were serious. It will be a wonderful wedding, and I have decided to make her dress. I can't wait to start."

"Oh, Paula, why go to all that work? Let's drive over to Knoxville together and see what we can find. I'd love to explore the bridal shops with you."

A disdainful look came over her face, "Have you looked at the wedding dresses these days? I went to Loveman's yesterday, and their dresses are just awful, sleazy fabric and badly made! I doubt whether Knoxville shops are any better, but I'll go take a look."

Paula's remark made me feel minimally cheered up. At least she was looking. All was not yet lost.

A couple of weeks went by before I saw Paula again. She called one afternoon, "Come on over. I want to show you what I found in Knoxville for Robin's wedding!" She sounded excited.

"Wedding dress, wedding dress, wedding dress..." I chanted to myself, fingers crossed for luck, as I walked across the yard to Paula's back door. "Hey, I'm here," I opened her door and stepped into her kitchen.

"Come on into the dining room," she called out.

I went into the dining room, hoping to see a dress hanging there. My heart sank as I looked around. Spread out on the dining room table lay yards and yards of beautiful heavy satin. Next to it, Paula had laid some antique Belgian lace that had been in her family for generations.

Smiling, she pulled out the pattern. "Look at this! Simple and elegant! It will be the perfect wedding dress my Robin deserves." She showed me the pattern.

I nodded, trying to think of something to say. Paula was right. It was a simple and elegant design, a classic wedding dress pattern, princess style with long sleeves. "I'll applique the lace around the neck of the dress, and there is enough to cover part of the bodice and shoulders. It will be gorgeous on this satin. I've already sent off a length of satin to have covered buttons made. Tell me, what do you think?"

"You are so right. It will be beautiful on Robin," I agreed. Then, hoping that she had at least bought the veil, I asked, "Did you buy a veil?"

"Oh no! Here, look at this lovely tulle! The veil will be a snap to make," she said, pulling out what looked to me like about a hundred yards of tulle. I looked from the tulle to the satin, with a feeling of despair at having failed Robin.

It would be a monumental job. I knew that working with satin is a slow and arduous task. All the stitching done on satin must be perfect the first time, because any changes will leave marks if stitches have to be ripped out and re-sewn. I found myself wishing that Paula had chosen lace for the dress.

Mistakes aren't noticeable on lace. A lace dress could be sewn very quickly and still look professional, even if stitches need to be changed.

Suddenly, I realized that my job description had abruptly changed: instead of trying to talk her out of making the wedding dress, now I needed to talk her into finishing it. Paula would need plenty of support and encouragement until the wedding was over. As the months went by, from time to time, a gentle nudge or two would be appropriate.

"Are you going to start right now?" I gave her my first gentle nudge.

"Oh no. Good Heavens, I don't need eleven months to make this dress. I'll wait for cooler weather. Then, I'll just organize everything carefully and stay on schedule." she smiled at me, "It'll work out beautifully."

The bride-to-be forgave me for being unable to stop her mother. "I really appreciate your trying, Bets. I sort of knew it was a lost cause from the beginning. Mother began talking about making my wedding dress the minute I told her that Steven and I were going to get married."

Summer ended and fall began. Paula told me she had begun to work on Robin's dress. It would be fun and an easy pattern to follow, she assured me. When Robin came home for Thanksgiving, they would check the fitting. I told her I knew it would be a professional job.

I called Paula from time to time, to see how it was going, but we didn't see much of each other that winter. Our kids went back to school; Becky and Melissa went away to school, and Brad went back to the Webb School in Knoxville. The bride-to-be returned to Duke to finish her senior year.

Whenever I ran into Harry, he told me that Paula was busy working on the dress. All was on target, he assured me, and her careful scheduling of the project was working out perfectly. I was always relieved to hear it was going well. I didn't go over to visit because I knew she didn't need interruptions. Now and then, I'd see her heading out to shop, and we'd stop and talk for a few minutes. She always seemed grateful for my encouragement and my praise of her sewing. I didn't have much of a chance to give her a regular allotment of nudges, but I decided that she really didn't need them.

May came, and I called Paula one day, and invited her family and out-of-town guests for dinner in the evening after the wedding. Robin and Steven were being married at 2 o'clock on Saturday in mid-June. From what Paula had told me, Steven's parents were difficult guests. They had visited earlier in the year when the two kids had announced their plans to marry. "They don't drink, they don't talk, they just sit there looking as if they disapproved of all of us," Paula confided. "Having dinner at your house will be heaven!"

"Great! We'll definitely do it," I said and added, "You can let me know the week before the wedding how many guests I should expect."

The dress was coming along well, she added. I felt a surge of relief.

The day of the wedding was a sunny, beautiful day. Early in the morning, I pulled on shorts and went outside to weed the garden. Dinner that night was pretty well organized, and I only needed to run down to Pine Valley shopping center to pick up a couple of last minute items.

I called to Art, "Let's walk down to Pine Valley. It'll feel good to stretch my legs after kneeling on the ground for the last couple of hours." Afterwards, I planned to relax in a hot bath, and let all the garden dirt soak off.

When we got to the grocery store, I wandered around picking up coffee cream, lettuce, and some other odds and ends. Just then, I looked up from my list and saw Harry. He was rushing around the store, a grim look on his face, picking up things then putting them down, pushing an empty cart around.

I went over to him, "Hi, Harry. How's everything going?"

He turned to me, a haunted look on his face, "The dress isn't finished!" he burst out. "Paula is frantic! She is trying to finish it." He looked at me.

"Harry, I'll go see what I can do to help Paula." I reminded him that they were all coming to dinner after the wedding.

Harry thought a moment, "It would be more help if you could bring lunch over. Paula is too busy to fix food for our guests and she didn't get to the store for food." He looked at me in desperation.

"Don't worry, Harry. You just drive me back to your house so I can work on the dress and Art can bring food over for lunch. Dinner tonight is all set, so this evening, you all can come over whenever you feel like it for dinner, as we had planned."

I grabbed Art, gave him a list of salad stuff, cheeses, fruit and good French bread, and asked him to take it all over to Harry and Paula's and arrange a nice buffet table for everyone. It would have to suffice for Robin's future in-laws as well as all the other out-of-town guests. They were all due to arrive momentarily at Paula's house, expecting to be entertained at lunch.

Then I turned back to Harry, "Come on, let's go, Harry," and we hurried out to his car.

The moment Harry drove into his driveway. I jumped out and ran into the house, and scrubbed my hands in the kitchen sink. Then, I gave Robin a hug and smiled, "Don't worry," I reassured her. After that, I asked Paula what needed to be done to finish the dress.

"Oh, dear..." she said, " The lace has to be appliqued to the dress, and the buttons need to be sewn down the back."

"What about the veil? Is that finished?" I asked.

"No, I still have to cut it out and iron the tulle," was the answer. Paula was now in an advanced stage of dithering. I needed to get her out of my way.

"Paula, tell me how you want the lace sewn on the dress, and give me the flowers for the veil. Put needles and thread, the buttons, the tulle and the lace here on the table. Now, you go take a bath and just leave me alone to get it done." I gave her a hug and a gentle push out the door.

Then I asked Robin to set up the ironing board and plug in the iron. "Please go have a bite of lunch, and just leave me alone. Oh, and spread a clean sheet on the floor under the ironing board. There isn't time to launder a dirty wedding dress."

I looked at the clock. It was one o'clock on the dot. The wedding was at two and it would take ten minutes to drive to the church. I had about thirty-five to forty minutes to finish the dress, cut out the tulle and make a veil, then iron both dress and veil.

Feeling like Rumpelstilskin, about to spin straw into gold, I got to work. First the functional: buttons were more essential than lace. Those were soon sewn on. Then I pinned the lace in place and I quickly tacked it on, so it would hold. I could sew it more carefully later.

I looked at the clock. It was one-ten. Thirty minutes left, I thought.

"I must do it all in twenty minutes, leaving time for them to dress," I mentally corrected my schedule. My heart was racing.

I pulled out the fabric for the veil, by now, a pile of very wrinkled tulle, laid it on the table and cut out the veil. Then I ironed it, and stitched the small cap of flowers on the top. "Hmmm… Not bad," I muttered to myself. Turning back to the dress, I started to sew the lace more securely, when there was a frantic cry from Paula, "I can't find my new brassiere!"

"Just a minute, I'll be right there," I called to her, glancing at the clock. It was now one twenty-five.

I dashed into the bedroom, looking through the clothes piled on the chairs, the dressers, and the unmade beds... no brassiere. Then, as I looked around at the chaos in the bedroom, I realized I hadn't look under the beds. Shoving the beds out from the wall, I got down on hands and knees and crawled into the corner, looking around on the floor beneath both beds. I could see clothes on the floor, so I pulled them out, dust bunnies and all. Aha! The new brassiere appeared, tag still hanging on, but not quite so pristine and clean as it might have been. I cut the tag off, shook off the dust, tossed it to Paula, and rushed back to my task. Sewing the lace on didn't take too long, but ironing the satin dress was slow work. I did it, but told myself that this was not the time to be too fussy. The hands of the clock were moving too fast. It was now one-thirty-five.

"We'll make it! We'll make it..."I muttered.

My heart pounding, I quickly called Robin, and helped her into her dress. Then I grabbed her older sister, Harriet, and asked her to button the dress up the back, while I finished ironing the veil. Glancing over, I prayed that I had sewn the buttons on securely enough.

Paula walked in, looking lovely in her pale blue mother-of-the-bride dress. I took one last look at Robin, dressed in her elegant wedding dress, the veil in place, and turned to her mother, "Great job, Paula. Your daughter looks like a princess in that beautiful dress!" I tossed kisses to them both, and dashed home.

I barely had time to pull on my dress, slide into my sandals, brush my hair, add lipstick and jump into the car with Art and the kids. The lovely Episcopal Church was nearly full, but we found space in a pew in the section with Robin's family. "If ever I belonged to a family, it's today," I thought. I felt like a cherished old family retainer "who had raised them babies …"

It was a beautiful wedding, and "my Robin" as I now thought of her, was a lovely bride, elegant in a satin dress with an applique of fragile old Belgian lace.

At the reception, when I went through the receiving line, Robin leaned close to me and whispered, "Well, you did it after all. "

"You mean I didn't do it, don't you? I couldn't talk her out of making it…"

"No, Bets, I mean you did do it… You managed to keep Mother from sewing up my dress as I walked down the aisle. The only thing is," she began to giggle, "I began to think it would be you who would be sewing me up as I walked down the aisle!"

Later, when I stopped to talk to Paula, she turned to look at Robin with misty eyes, as she said, "Doesn't she look lovely in that beautiful dress? I told Harry, it was the best decision I ever made, to make her wedding dress myself!"

Garden Tour

The airport limousine was filled the night I flew home from a visit to my sister in Michigan. It was now past midnight, and the passengers heading to Oak Ridge were exhausted. Most of them were visiting scientists who were coming to attend a conference at the Oak Ridge National Laboratory. Due to bad thunderstorms in the area of the Knoxville airport, where our flight terminated, we had been delayed on takeoff. Luckily, when the limousine drove up, I grabbed the passenger seat next to the driver, and was able to tilt it back, close my eyes, and relax.

During the drive to Oak Ridge from the Knoxville airport, the passengers were quiet, just two of them talking quietly. We were all tired and out of sorts due to the delay. I noticed one or two of the visitors dozing, and I envied them the ability to sleep in such uncomfortable circumstances.

Suddenly, one of the men in the back row, who had been talking quietly to his neighbor, spoke up in a loud voice, obviously addressing all of us passengers, "I haf a beautifool dahlia garden in Oak Ridge, and many unusual varieties that von does not offen see. They are chust now plooming and veddy beautifool. I think, Driver, that everyone mos come to see my garden."

Suddenly, I thought I recognized Dr. Gunter Barna, whom I had seen at a Biology Division reception. He was a well known scientist and avid gardener.

"Yassuh," said the driver, looking back in his rear-view mirror, "Folks kin go on by yo house, if you jes gives 'em yo address, suh." The African-American driver appeared nervous, as he spoke, and I saw a look of apprehension on his face as I glanced at him.

"Oh, no, Driver, they mos come tonight so I can gif tour and tell about history of each variety."

The driver just laughed, somewhat uneasily, I thought. It was clear he hoped that Dr. Barna was just joking.

"Do you know Dr. Barna?" I asked the driver quietly.

"Oh, yas ma'am. An Ah bin down this heah road befoa." I was puzzled by his remark, but didn't question him further.

I turned and looked back and saw the assembled passengers, now completely awakened by Dr. Barna's loud lecture, muttering to each other, most of them trying to settle down and doze off again.

Dr. Barna raised his voice and spoke again, "Now ees perfect time of year to see my dahlias at peak of ploom. Later, too hot. You vill loff vat I vill show to you ven ve get to my house."

When we finally arrived at the outskirts of Oak Ridge, Dr. Barna insisted that the limousine driver change his established pattern of dropping passengers off. It was the custom to begin at the east end of town, and first take passengers who lived in the area of streets whose names began with first letters of the alphabet. Anyone living on one of the streets just off California Avenue was taken home before someone living on Pennsylvania Avenue, where Art and I lived.

Dr. Barna ordered the poor driver to stop at his house first. "I vill get flashlights, so efree von can see plooms like daylight!"

The poor driver tried to tell Barna that it was now 1 o'clock in the morning, and he was responsible for getting passengers home and to the hotel.

"Dunt vorry," was the airy reply, "Chust ask the passengers und they vill tell you how vonderful vill be this garden tour."

I sat there in my front seat, convulsed with laughter, as I watched Dr. Barna begin his garden tour. There was no doubt

124

that this man, small and slight as he was, was the stuff of successful dictators, or at least field marshals.

Fifty-five minutes later we saw Dr. Barna returning with his captive visitors to the limousine. They climbed in, muttering and cursing.

"Have you driven Dr. Barna before?" I quietly asked the exhausted driver.

"Oh, Ma'am, I shore bin lucky." He rolled his eyes at me. "The Doctor's ridden with me three tahms befo', and ever tahm he takes the pore passengers prisoner to show 'em somethin' real special. Las tahm hit was some special bred mice he was proud of. He had them mice in his briefcase durin' the whole trip, he said. He puts it under the passenger seat, opened up jes a little, so them mice kin git fresh air. An, smell! Lawd hep us, did them things smell!"

"An Ma'am, that tahm, I heah someone ax Dr. Barna did he git hassled by the airline about them smelly mice," Then the driver turned to me with a big grin and whispered, "An you ain't goin' bleeve this, but the Doctor he say that the airlines never give him no trouble because he always puts his briefcase underneath someone else's seat!"

Pretty Kitty

I sat, pencil in hand reading over my list of errands. "Check on Art's passport, take Brad for his pre-camp physical, then go say goodbye to Leslie before she leaves for the Peace Corps, what else is there?"

I smiled as I thought about Leslie, our next-door neighbor Martha's daughter. We had watched her grow up from a shy little nine year old to a charming young woman, just out of college. I felt so happy that she had not cancelled her Peace Corps plans when her father died four months ago. Some of her mother's friends had told her she should give up her dream and stay home and take care of her mother.

When I heard that, I told Leslie not to listen to what they said "You must go, Leslie. The best thing you can do for your mother is to leave her now and give her a chance to become independent."

So today Leslie was flying to Honolulu. She would live on one of the remote Hawaiian Islands for training. There she would be enrolled in an intensive language program before going to her assignment in Korea.

I was drinking my second cup of coffee and going over my list when Martha telephoned. "Come on down and see what we have here."

"What is it?" I asked.

"We have a lion visiting."

"What? We'll be right down!" Excitedly, I called Melissa and Brad and we rushed down the hill to Martha's house next door.

There in the front yard was a young man with a gorgeous young lioness on a leash. She was a tawny, sleek beauty, muscles rippling as she tugged on the heavy leash, pulling her caretaker around as she explored the yard.

Martha and her kids stood there watching, taking care to keep some 10 or 15 feet away from the lion.

Martha introduced Melissa, Brad and me to the young man with the lion. "Betsy," she said, "this is Tom. He and Leslie have been friends since the summer they both worked at Mammoth Cave."

Tom called a hello to us and continued to walk around with the big cat.

"How'd you get this job, Tom?" I asked.

"Leslie," he called, "tell Mrs. Upton and her kids why I'm doing this." He had an endearing grin on his face.

"There is a funny story around this," Leslie was laughing as she came over to talk to us. "Tom graduated last year from Tulane, and he got a great job working for Holiday Inn in Atlanta. Then Columbia Pictures decided to do a publicity stunt for their movie, *Born Free*, which just opened, you know. They wanted someone who could travel around this summer with a lion, to the cities where the movie is opening. They were looking for someone with experience handling lions and someone told them about Tom."

"Where did he learn to handle lions?" I asked Leslie.

"The summer before we met at Mammoth Cave, he had a job with a small circus and learned how to handle lions and tigers. When the studio heard about him, they contacted him to see if he would work for them. They are paying him a lot of money to do the publicity. Plus, they fitted out that Land Rover for the lion and they pay for his hotels and meals."

"Did he take a leave of absence from the Holiday Inn?" I asked.

"Well, that was the problem. He knew he couldn't ask for a summer off when he just started working for them last year. He really likes the job with Holiday Inn, and doesn't want to lose it. But he knew it would be a lot of fun spending the summer working with a lion."

"Quick!" I laughed, "Don't leave me in suspense! How did he work it out?"

"Well, he told his boss at work that his grandmother was very sick, and he wanted the summer off to be with her. He has a sympathetic boss who gave him the time off." She lowered her voice. "He feels embarrassed about telling the lie, but he really wanted the publicity job."

Martha had walked over and joined Leslie and me. She said, "Leslie says that Tom isn't his real name. He's using a fake name while he works with the lion, so the Holiday Inn people won't recognize him if something shows up in the paper about the Born Free publicity. Sometimes they take pictures of the lion when he is showing her off."

I kept watching the beautiful young animal. What fun it would be to be able to handle a big cat like her.

"Tom," I called, "Is she dangerous? Would it be safe to pet her?"

"Oh, absolutely!" he replied. "She is used to people, and there wouldn't be any risk in petting her. Come on over, if you want to."

I couldn't resist. I walked quietly over to where Tom was standing with the young beauty, on the lawn, and reached out to gently pet her. For a moment, I stroked her head, admiring her. Suddenly, she turned, snarling at me and sank her teeth into my upper arm! Tom reacted immediately. Grabbing the lion's head, he worked to force her jaws open, and after a few minutes, she let my arm go.

Tom was horrified and very apologetic. He hurriedly took the lion, over to the Land Rover, and put her into the cage in the back. Then he came over to look at my arm. It bled quite a bit, but she had not torn the flesh, so it was not a serious injury.

Tom was terribly upset with himself. "She's never done

anything like that, and I never would have let you come near if I thought she was dangerous."

I felt just as apologetic for my own actions. "That was really stupid of me, and I am sorry." I tried to reassure the contrite young man. "Don't worry about it, it's not serious. I've been bitten by cats before, these were just bigger teeth."

Leslie was ready to leave. Tom was giving her a ride to the airport. "Gosh, Betsy, are you really O.K.? I hate to say goodbye to you just after you get bitten by my friend's lion!" Leslie and I hugged goodbye, as I told her not to worry about me. She got a little tearful as she whispered in my ear, "Thank you so much for telling me to go."

"You lucky dog!" I teased her, "Going to one of the Hawaiian islands to learn Korean! Lying around on the beach while you learn a new language! What could be better?" Then I added as I hugged her, "The Peace Corps is lucky to be getting you."

Melissa, Brad and I walked back up the hill to our house, where I scrubbed my arm, and wiped it off with alcohol. The bites were deep, but soon stopped bleeding.

Sometime later, the phone rang. It was Art. "Don't forget to get my passport from the Bank Box." He was abrupt, rushing to get ready to fly to Austria the following day. "How is your day? Everything O.K.?"

"Yeah, I'm O.K. now, but a lion bit me this morning."

"That's nice, I'll see you this evening." He hung up.

Twenty minutes later, the phone ran again, "What did you say? Something about a lion?" Art asked.

I told him what had happened, but assured him that I was fine. He was in a rush getting ready for his conference. After the Austrian meeting, when Melissa went to music camp and Brad went to camp in North Carolina, I planned to meet Art in Cortina, Italy, where he was scheduled to attend another scientific meeting.

Later Martha called, also concerned about my lion bite, and I told her it was nothing to worry about. She was feeling sad at having seen her eldest daughter depart, happy though she was about Leslie joining the Peace Corps. "It was a pretty dramatic kind of send-off," she laughed. "Having Tom arrive unexpectedly with a lion. Leslie was laughing about it, after we all knew that you were O.K."

The following morning I took Brad to Dr. Wallace for his physical. In the course of our conversation, I told him that a lion had bitten me the day before. He insisted on taking a look, and agreed that the bite was nothing to worry about. However, he added, "You must find out whether that lion has a current rabies shot. You can't go off to Italy unless you make sure before you go. If you wait until your return, it would be too late to get rabies treatment." He was very insistent about this.

I called Martha as soon as we got home and asked how I could get in touch with Tom. She was dismayed, "Betsy, Leslie never told me what his real name is and I don't even know what last name he is using this summer. Besides, he didn't say where he was going after he left."

"Can I contact Leslie and ask her?"

"I don't have any way to reach her, either. The Peace Corps didn't let its new recruits know where they were going, and Leslie was told that nobody could call her once her training began. Of course, when her training is finished, we'll be back in contact again. But that won't be until October."

I realized the dilemma I was in. Both Leslie and Tom were on another planet, and I had no way to reach either one.

I sat there by the phone staring into space. What had seemed merely an impulsive act on my part could actually become something far more serious. Just then the phone rang. It was Becky, who was working as a counselor at a Michigan camp.

"Hi, Mom. I have a break, so I thought I'd call and see how everything is at home. Is Brad excited about the North Carolina camp? And when does Melissa leave for music camp? I want her address so I can write her while she's there."

We talked a few minutes, then I called the kids to talk to Becky. I heard Melissa say goodbye to Becky, and then she called me, "Mom, she wants to talk to you again."

"Mom! Why didn't you tell me about the lion bite?" Becky burst out.

I started to reassure her, but then told her I wasn't able to find out about the rabies shot because I couldn't contact either Leslie or Tom. It seemed as though they had virtually vanished off the face of the earth.

"O.K., Mom, just listen to me. Here's what you do. Call Columbia Pictures in Hollywood to find out where that lion came from. But be sure you reverse the charge. That's the only way you can get their attention. Do you remember those shoes I was trying to return to the company last year, from school, when they sent the wrong size? I paid for the first call, and got a brush off. Then, I reversed the charge, and boy, did that make a difference! Of course, I also hinted that my uncle is a lawyer. You might add that line, too."

"Darling! What a genius I produced! I'll do it immediately!" We laughed together. At 15, Becky had more common sense than most of my forty-something friends.

As soon as we hung up, I put through a call to the head of publicity at Columbia Pictures, in Hollywood. Before the receptionist would accept the call, she asked what business I represented and why I was calling. I told the receptionist that I was bitten by their lion, and wanted to talk to the director of publicity about it. She replied in a haughty Brooklyn accent that Columbia Pictures didn't do any publicity and besides, they didn't have any lions and hung up.

I immediately called back. "Why are you calling again?"

asked the receptionist in a pompous voice. "I told you, we don't have any lions."

"Columbia Pictures has just released a film, *Born Free*. Have you heard of it?" I used my sweetest, most sarcastic voice. "Now, some publicity person at Columbia arranged to publicize the movie by having a lion taken around to attract attention to the movie. That lion has bitten me and I must speak to the head of publicity at Columbia Pictures about it." I added that if she didn't think it was important, I could ask...

"Just a minute," she hastily interrupted me. I sensed that the word "lawyer" might be floating around in her mind.

"This is Michael Lewis speaking. What can we do for you?" a man's voice spoke.

I told him what had happened, and that I had been advised to find out about the lion's rabies shots.

"Our office is not involved in publicity for individual films. Another department is responsible," Michael Lewis's voice was gentle and soothing as he reassured me. "But don't worry, Mrs. Upton. I will find out about it and get back to you immediately."

We hung up and I sat there, laughing as I thought about Becky and her shoe experience. Later that day when she called to check up on my progress, I told her that she should start a column, "Advice to Muddled Mothers."

The following morning, at nine o'clock, the phone rang.

"Mrs. Upton," a man's voice greeted me. "This is Stanley Rossman, calling from Atlanta. I am very sorry to hear that my cat bit you."

Relief surged through me. "Mr. Rossman, what a relief to hear your voice. I feel so stupid about petting your pretty kitty, but the young handler thought she was gentle enough for me to do it."

I explained that I hadn't been seriously injured, and had been inclined to forget it, but that our pediatrician had worried me with his concern about rabies.

"You don't have to give another thought to rabies, Mrs. Upton," Mr. Rossman assured me, "nor do you have to worry about lion fever. She's had all her shots."

I laughed, and said, "Hmm, I'll have to tell our pediatrician that he missed one possibility. It never occurred to either of us that I might get lion fever."

He then told me that the young lion had been a pet, and had been gentle up to now. But beginning at this age, there was always uncertainty about a big cat's behavior. They were potentially dangerous animals, especially in unfamiliar situations.

"I've raised several big cats," he explained. "I've had tigers, lions and once a leopard. When they are grown and become dangerous, I give them to a zoo where they don't keep them in cages but where they have a lot of space for them to roam, like the Bronx Zoo in New York. But you liked my pretty kitty, didn't you?"

"She's gorgeous!" I replied. "I couldn't resist her."

"Why don't you come on down to Atlanta for a visit and I'd be delighted to show you my newest big cat. I'd like to meet the lady who couldn't resist petting one of my kitties."

"What a wonderful invitation, Mr. Rossman. I'd like nothing better."

I regret to say that I never got to Atlanta.

Mr. Rossman, if you ever read this, please give me a call so I can take you up on your invitation. I've postponed it far too long.

The Snake Did It

"The snake was responsible," I always insisted, for years afterwards. Art disagreed, "It wasn't the snake, it was you. You did it."

That morning at breakfast, the whole family was keyed up. Brad and I were the first to sit down to eat, both of us dressed in jeans, heavy shirts and sturdy hiking shoes. His fifth grade class was going to spend the day deep in the Tennessee woods and I was going along as one of several assistants to help the teacher keep order. Each year, Mrs. Keese, Brad's teacher, arranged to have three scientists meet with her class for a day of hands-on science in the woods. There was an arborist to teach the children about trees, a botanist who would focus on plants and an entomologist, whose specialty was insect life. At noon, we assistants would build a fire and the kids would help us cook lunch for the crowd.

Brad was excited about the day, and pleased that I was going along.

That morning, both girls were also keyed up. Melissa was scheduled to give her first chapel talk at school. The Webb School, a private country day school in Knoxville, required all students to give one chapel talk each year on any subject the student chose. Melissa, who was a new seventh-grader at Webb, immediately decided to talk about her interest in herpetology and begged us to let her take Brighty, our pet corn snake, to school to show to the audience of students and teachers.

Art and I were uneasy about the snake going to school, fearful that he might get loose, so we said, "No!"

However, Becky immediately defended Melissa's eagerness to take the snake to show during her talk. She strongly supported her sister's idea, saying, "Her talk will be really great if she can show everyone the snake. The whole school will pay attention. Besides, I'll help if Brighty gets loose. Just don't worry."

So, still somewhat reluctantly, Art and I finally agreed to Melissa's request. "All right, darling," I said. "You may carry Brighty in my big Italian straw bag. The soft cotton lining will make it comfortable for him and air will circulate through the straw. But, you must promise not to open the bag anywhere except in the auditorium during your chapel talk. Do not open it on the bus."

Excited, Melissa threw her arms around me as she promised.

That morning, Art was also somewhat preoccupied about the conference he was hosting at the Biology Division. The topic, "Radiation Injury" had generated a large response. Some 85 to 90 scientists were expected to attend from all areas of the U.S and abroad.

We had invited the visiting scientists to come to an informal dinner party that evening, following the opening conference. I had not expected the party to be the same day as the Day in the Woods, but I wasn't concerned about it. We entertained visitors frequently, so I had spent the day before cooking the food for the party.

There would be plenty of time to return from the woods with Brad, go pick up both girls at the Pine Valley stop when the Webb School van dropped them off, and take them to their music lessons.

The Day in the Woods was a memorable experience. Driving back to pick up the girls at the end of the day, Brad and I talked about our wonderful day. I dropped him off at home and drove to meet the girls at the bus stop.

As I turned into the Pine Valley parking lot, I saw the Webb School van parked there, and Chris Maynard, the young Latin teacher, who drove it, standing there with Becky and Melissa. Both girls were sobbing as I walked over.

"Oh, Mom," Melissa said, "Brighty got out on the bus and now he's tangled up under the back seat. He may be hurt or dead!"

"How did this happen?" I asked Melissa. "How could the snake get out of a locked purse?"

Melissa began to cry even harder. Between sobs she admitted that she had opened the big bag on the bus after the older boys teased her. "They said I was afraid of the snake and so I had to show them I wasn't."

I wrapped my arms around Melissa and told the girls, "Don't worry, darlings. Just wait, I'll get our Brighty out of the bus right now."

I turned to Chris Maynard and asked if he could wait a few minutes so I could get the snake out of the bus. However, the young teacher apologized that he could not wait for me to rescue the snake from the bus as he had an urgent appointment in Knoxville and had to get back to Webb School as soon as possible.

As soon as I realized that I would have to drive over to Knoxville, I told both girls to walk to their music lessons, and then walk home afterwards.

Then I turned back to Chris Maynard and asked, "Are you afraid of snakes? If so, you can drive my car and I'll drive the van back to Webb."

He assured me that he was not nervous about the snake, so he climbed into the van and drove off. I followed him back to the school, a trip of about 35 minutes.

When we got back to Webb, the young teacher parked the van and opened the back door so I could get in, apologizing profusely for having to leave me. On hands and knees I crawled down the aisle of the van looking for our beloved snake. He had vanished from beneath the back seat and I had to get out and go grab a flashlight from my car to find him. Brighty had chosen the darkest corner to coil himself around the springs under another seat.

Soothingly, I rubbed his head and ran my warm hand down his back, as I slowly and gently untangled our pet. Once he was free, I looped him twice around my neck as I started for the door of the van.

I was about to step down from the van when a gentle voice spoke, "Mrs. Upton, I'd like you to meet my wife."

There was Robert Webb, the headmaster standing next to the door of the van. Evidently, Mr. Maynard had alerted him to the problem.

I stepped down from the van, both hands stroking the nervous snake.

"How do you do?" Mrs. Webb and I greeted one another, however, without shaking hands. Julie Webb was a lovely young woman, the epitome of a gracious Southern lady, dressed in a pink tweed suit, a faint scent of Chanel #5 about her, and a string of pearls around her neck.

I was instantly aware of my own dirty clothes, smelling of wood smoke, as I stood there. Instead of pearls, I had six feet of corn snake around my neck.

I drove home with Brighty safely tucked into my big Italian bag. The kids rushed out to greet me, and Melissa started to cry again, thankful that our pet snake was safe at home. I hugged and kissed all three kids, and then got ready for the dinner.

I quickly washed my face, sprayed Chanel #5 behind my ears, threw on a long skirt and blouse, and we all had a great time at our dinner party.

Six months later on a sunny April afternoon, I drove to Webb School for a tea for the parents. I was dressed in a blue tweed suit, a spritz of Chanel #5 behind my ears, with pearls at my ears and around my neck.

As I moved along the receiving line, I came to Julie Webb, the headmaster's charming wife. "Mrs. Webb," I smiled, "I am Betsy Upton. Our daughters Rebecca and Melissa are new students this year."

Mrs. Webb burst out laughing as she shook my hand, "Oh, Mrs. Upton, you don't need to introduce yourself! I'll never forget you. You're the lady with the snake!"

Six months afterwards, the phone rang, "Mrs. Upton, this is Robert Webb. I am calling to invite you to become a member of the Board of Trustees of the Webb School of Knoxville."

Stunned, but delighted, I accepted the honor and served as a Trustee for three years. It was such an interesting experience that I blessed the snake every time I thought about it.

Because, I still say, the snake did it. Draped around my neck, our beautiful corn snake got me elected to the Board of Trustees of the Webb School of Knoxville. A string of pearls just would not have done it.

Shhhhhh ...

During the nineteen years Art worked at the Oak Ridge National Laboratory in east Tennessee, there was a steady stream of scientists who came to visit. The focus of his research at the Lab was the effects of radiation. This was a field of enormous interest after the war, so Oak Ridge became a major peacetime scientific center, attracting visitors from all over the world.

Both Art and I enjoyed the visitors, and we made it a habit to entertain them all at dinner, sometimes alone, but more often inviting several other guests in the same or similar fields.

One day in March, Art mentioned that Professor Karol Frantisek, an eminent biologist from Czechoslovakia, would be visiting his lab for a weekend in April. He would be our first visitor from behind the Iron Curtain, and it would be an interesting visit.

We decided to plan a special dinner party for him, so Art began to make up a guest list for a dinner party. As the date of his visit drew near, we invited five or six of Art's colleagues from the lab, whom he knew would be interested in meeting the Czech scientist.

Then, on the Wednesday, just two days before Professor Frantisek was scheduled to arrive, Art came home, with a puzzled look on his face.

"I've had the strangest telephone call from the Atomic Energy Commission this afternoon. They told me that we have to have Professor Frantisek spend the weekend at our house, not at the hotel. We must keep him under surveillance the entire time he is here. We have to cancel our dinner party, and keep him away from anyone outside of the family. I kept asking what the reason was, and they just said it was top secret, and nobody was to know. The other thing they were definite about was that he was not to watch television, nor listen to the radio, nor read any newspapers or magazines. It was a weird conversation."

"Art, do you suppose he is some kind of spy?"

Art just laughed, "From what I know of the man's outstanding scientific reputation, he is too busy turning out first rate research to spend time moonlighting as a spy!" We both laughed.

"Now, I don't want to upset you, but the A.E.C. man who called also advised us to put away anything personal that we wouldn't want to have fall into the wrong hands. He said that we should gather up financial records, letters, bills paid and unpaid, and hide it all away. Frankly, I don't get this part of it."

"Wait a minute, Art! I've read enough mysteries and spy thrillers to know he must think we have incriminating personal stuff that we could be blackmailed about! Do you realize that? What the dickens are we getting into the middle of?" Then I began to laugh, "Hey, you know what? This is going to be great fun. I've only read whodunits, now I get to live through a weekend of wondering who-dun-what?"

We both whipped into action to arrange the guestroom for Professor Frantisek. In addition to being our kids playroom, and occasional guestroom, this room also functioned as my study with my desk, with bills and correspondence filed in the desk drawer.

Art went off to telephone our guests and tell them that the dinner party was cancelled, while I began to stuff large plastic garbage bags with the contents of my desk. In went old letters, old bills, current bills just paid, as well as some current bills, as yet unpaid. I could easily retrieve the latter to pay after our guest left. I carried three bags of papers to the attic crawl space and put them into a corner. The checkbook was tucked into the back of the closet in our bedroom. I doubted that our visitor would be interested in nosing around on our closet floor.

Two days later, on Friday, we looked at each other uneasily, when the airport shuttle stopped in front, and we walked out to greet Professor Frantisek. To our relief, he was not some kind of Iron Curtain thug, but a charming, cultured man, with a wide range of interests. Far from appearing suspicious. about the sudden changes in his visit, he seemed delighted to be a guest in our home.

Each morning, I tiptoed out the front door, grabbed the newspaper, and tossed it into the garbage can. The TV and radios were stashed in one of the kitchen cupboards. I wondered whether Karol Frantisek thought we were totally uninterested in world affairs, with nothing at all to read in the house.

It was a fruitful visit for Art, and the two men spent two days in Art's lab sharing research information. On Monday, when the limousine came to take our delightful guest to the airport, we felt sorry to see our new friend depart.

We said goodbye, then Art and I looked at each other.

"What was that all about?" I asked. "What danger was there from that charming man?"

On Monday, April 17 when Art came home from work, he told me that Cuba was being attacked by CIA-trained Cuban defectors. The Bay of Pigs was one of the targets of the bombings, and the proposed target of landings.

We looked at each other. "Art, did the AEC really worry that our Czech visitor might contact the Cubans if he had known what was going on? What kind of paranoia do they suffer from, anyway?" We stood there half amused, but half shocked at the same time..

Several years passed. In 1969, Art and I were packing up

in preparation for our move to the State University of New York at Stony Brook, on Long Island.

Back in a corner of the attic crawlspace were three large plastic garbage bags. What could they be?

When I took them downstairs to open them, I burst out laughing. All of our dangerous papers, letters, and bills were piled in front of me. Had we missed any of them or needed them during the past eight years? Not a single one. However, as a memento of a mysterious weekend with our Iron Curtain visitor in 1961, and as a reminder of our country's case of Red Hysteria, they were an evocative pile of papers, yellowed and brittle.

The Great Mosquito Massacre

During the years our children were growing up in Oak Ridge, Art was too busy to take family trips with the kids and me. In addition to his demanding work schedule, he traveled frequently to scientific meetings. So, for him, taking an extra trip with the family just for fun did not look like fun to him. Besides, Art never took his full vacation allotment. Unlike his colleagues who chose to forget about work for two or three weeks each year, Art preferred to just add a day or two to an occasional weekend each year.

However, whenever the subject of a family trip came up, Art always insisted that there was one important family trip we should take. We must take our three children and drive west, to the great natural sites like Yellowstone, the Grand Tetons, the Grand Canyon, and Mesa Verde. We both agreed to wait until they were all old enough to enjoy the long drive west.

In the meantime, while they were still quite young, I used to drive north with them to Michigan every year to visit my mother, my sister Nan and her family, and Art's parents. On our first trip, seven year old Becky, quickly became a skilled navigator, watching for road signs. She was especially helpful when I was driving through unfamiliar towns and she always kept me from making wrong turns or running red lights. Melissa and Brad, who were five and three years old on that first trip, were seat-belted in back, playing noisy road games or tickling each other, to gales of laughter.

Later, as the years went by, and the kids were in school, my mother used to come south to visit in the spring when Art was away at meetings. Twice, her visits coincided with our children's spring breaks, so with no prior plan, Mom, the kids and I just jumped into the car and drove to Florida to enjoy beach life. I have wonderful memories of our living like a bunch of beachcombers for a whole week.

Then, one evening in January, 1964, after the kids had gone to bed, I tapped Art on the shoulder, and asked "Do you know what year this is?"

He looked puzzled and asked, "What do you mean?"

"I just want to bring it to your attention that this is the perfect year to take our great western family trip. Remember how we agreed to wait until they were the right ages to take a long car trip?"

"Oh no!" Art started, "This is going to be a very busy year for me. I don't see how I can get away..."

"Oh, Art, you can't let them down now. They are at the ages we told them we would take our trip west. Brad is twelve, Melissa is fourteen and Becky is sixteen. They are all thrilled that Daddy is finally going on a trip with them. I don't think you realize how much this means to all three of them. Please clear your calendar this once and make time for the family."

Art finally agreed, so the two of us looked over the calendar and picked a date toward the end of June for us to start west. Every night at dinner, the five of us began to talk about the places we wanted to visit and the sites we looked forward to seeing.

"The Painted Desert or maybe Monument Valley, I think that's where they make cowboy movies," Brad said. "Can we go there? We might see them making a movie."

"I can't wait to see the Grand Canyon," Becky added, "Will we have time to take a boat ride through the canyon or maybe ride on a burro down from the top? Burros are supposed to be very sure-footed on steep trails like that one."

Melissa giggled as she added, "Nancy told me that Yellowstone has these spurts of water that make noises like 'Blurp, Blurp!' And the water smells yucky! Like rotten eggs!" She

144

made a face and we all began to laugh.

All that spring we made our plans, where to go, how long to stay in each place, what food to take along for picnics along the way, what toys and games to take in the car for fun on long days of driving.

Then, the night before we were scheduled to depart, Art came home from work and announced that he would not be able to go with us. He had just found out about an important scientific conference at the United Nations. Dr. Hollaender, the Biology Division director, had suggested that Art ought to go.

"Can't you tell him we have a family trip planned? Can't someone else go?" I asked.

But Art had never been to the United Nations and he admitted that he didn't want to miss this meeting. "We'll take our family trip next summer," he promised.

"No, we are going tomorrow," I replied. "Next summer will be too late."

"What? You can't go alone!"

"Wanna bet? We'll be halfway to Nashville before your limousine gets to the Knoxville airport. Listen, as you know, the kids are just at the right age to travel this summer. Brad is twelve, old enough to really enjoy the trip. All I have to do with him is stop the car now and then and let him run to the top of a hill and back, to let him work off his energy. Melissa is fourteen, she is the perfect age to travel with. In fact, she is the perfect age for anything at all. Becky is sixteen, and this is the perfect summer for her to travel. Please understand that word 'sixteen.' What 'sixteen' means is that her family is still OK, or at least tolerable, most of the time. In another year she won't even like any of us and wouldn't be caught dead traveling with us. So don't waste your breath, Art. We're going, with you or without you."

"I don't like the idea of you going alone. You don't even

have anyone to share the driving."

"Sure I do. Becky will share the driving with me. She's an excellent driver. I should know. I was the one who taught her to drive. I really wish you were going with us. We all looked forward to having you with us on this trip, but we don't really need you to go along."

The case closed, Art accepted my decision. He would meet us in Denver in mid-July and we would all spend a week together in Aspen, where he was scheduled to attend a scientific meeting. After that, he would be free, and we'd all drive to Mesa Verde and then visit the other sites we wanted to see on the way home.

The following morning, the first week of July, Becky, Melissa, Brad and I piled into the car and headed west, all of us excited. It was a beautiful sunny Tennessee June morning as we headed west on I-40. I drove for a couple of hours, and then pulled off the highway.

"What's wrong, Mom?" Becky looked apprehensively at me.

"Nothing's wrong, Darling. I'm just ready to have a rest, so we'll change places and you can take over the driving."

I walked around the car, grabbed a pillow from the middle seat of the station wagon, and got into the passenger seat. "Wake me up in two hours," I said to Becky. She looked stunned as I tilted my seat back as far as it would go, stuck the pillow behind my head, closed my eyes and fell asleep immediately.

Becky later told me that she looked at me, sound asleep, then turned around and looked at her younger sister and brother in the back seat, and said to herself, "Mom really trusts me! She trusts me to be responsible for taking care of Melissa and Brad and her." Of course she didn't tell me that summer how she had felt. Sixteen is not the age when you tell your mother that she did something that was O.K. It was several years before Becky told me that giving her that responsibility had made her both proud and happy.

But then, we were both reluctant to share our innermost thoughts, at that point. Did I tell her why I went to sleep so fast? Of course I didn't. How could I tell my sixteen year old daughter, a brand new driver, that the only way I was able to get used to her driving on major highways, was to be sound asleep when she took the wheel?

Our trip west was a dream trip. We saw everything we wanted to see. Anytime anyone wanted to stop and explore some trading post gift shop along the way, we stopped. Anytime the kids wanted to explore a hill, we stopped and they ran up and back. We listened to the kids' favorite rock music, full blast on the radio, as we drove down the highway. We stopped along the way to picnic wherever we felt like it. I was determined that this trip was for the kids, and whatever interested them, we took the time to look at.

When I was a child, driving with my parents to a new place, anytime my sister Nanny and I begged to stop and see something, Carlsbad Caverns, the Grand Canyon, or a trading post, the answer was always "We'll stop next time." However, the next time never came.

We laughed as spiffy new cars, all air-conditioned, passed us, giving us the finger and sneering at our ten-year old Ford station-wagon. Our car just chugged up mountain roads like the little engine "that could." Many times we had the last laugh when we passed those new cars stuck on the shoulder, overheated or with vapor lock.

To me it was important to let the kids have as much fun as possible on such a long trip. When we got to Hays, Kansas, the heat was so unbearable that I decided to stop earlier than usual and drove around the town until I found a motel with a nice swimming pool. Later, as we sat on the side of the pool, now wet and cool, I jokingly asked how they would like it if their dad decided to take a job in Kansas. The three of them looked at me in horror. "Don't worry" I grinned, "If Daddy took a job here, I would divorce him on the basis of incompatibility. I am not compatible with Kansas in the summertime."

We laughed and jumped back into the pool.

Yellowstone National Park was our next destination. We were all a bit road-weary, and I knew it would be a wonderful change to be able to spend several days exploring the area and doing some walking.

We drove up to the entrance to Yellowstone mid-afternoon on Friday, July the third and I stopped and waited for the attendant.

"Good afternoon, Ma'am. Please show me your reservation."

"Reservation?" I asked. "What do you mean, my reservation?"

"Ma'am, you have to have a reservation for the place you have reserved to stay. That's what I need to see."

In desperation, I pulled out the half-forgotten remnants of my Louisiana accent, and looked up at the attendant in despair, "Oh, mah! I didn't have inny idea I needed a reservation, no suh! We jes drove all the way from Eas Tinnissee, and this place is so fah away from ever'thing, I had no idea it might be crowded. Oh deah! What kin I do now?"

"Ma'am, don't you realize this is the fourth of July weekend and Yellowstone is full up? I doubt whether there is even space in the campgrounds."

My eyes filled up with tears, partly from fatigue and partly from a contact lens that suddenly went off center making my eyes water. The attendant looked at me with pity, and said, "Tell you what, Ma'am. You wait a few minutes, while I go see what I can do."

We sat there, and about five minutes he came back, saying "You are really in luck, Ma'am. There was one cabin that was just vacated, so you can have it for a week." He gave us a key and directions to the cabin, and with a grin, added, "And the next time you drive all the way from Tennessee, please Ma'am, call and get a reservation before you start out." I thanked him profusely and drove to the cabin we had just been assigned.

It was a rustic cabin, with a screen door standing half opened, and inside it smelled like a pine forest. As soon as we unloaded the car, and closed the cabin door, I looked around and burst out laughing. The cabin was full of mosquitoes that had clearly driven away the poor family who had reserved it for the holiday weekend. When the kids looked at me, I explained my amusement. "Do you know who we have to thank for this cabin being suddenly available? Look at all these mosquitoes. They all have bright red bellies, so they have just filled themselves up biting the people who reserved this cabin. O.K. kids, it's war. Take off your sandals and let's kill them all! Take no prisoners!"

The four of us spent about an hour, killing every mosquito in the cabin, smashing them against the walls, on the white bedspreads, on the furniture. When we finished, the walls dripped with bright red blood. The entire cabin was splattered with blood from those engorged mosquitos.

I got up on a chair and posed like a field marshal, "Attention, my darlings. We have won the war. The great mosquito massacre is over and we are the victors! However, I think we owe a cheer of thanks to our enemy for getting rid of the people who reserved this cabin and who were forced to retreat by the mosquito army. We will sleep in peace tonight without a single mosquito attack."

Lost and Found in the Holiday Inn

We were homeward bound. The kids and I were driving back to Tennessee after our great Western trip. We were at the end of six weeks of fun and laughter as we visited Yellowstone, Jackson Hole, Aspen, Mesa Verde, the Grand Canyon, the Painted Desert and last of all, Santa Fe, New Mexico, where we stopped to see my cousin Dave and his family. They lived in an old stagecoach inn, an historic New Mexican bit of architecture, shared by several colonies of spiders.

Art finally joined us at the Denver airport where we picked him up. He was going to a conference in Aspen while the kids and I looked forward to exploring the area and enjoying ourselves for the week on a ranch just outside of Aspen.

Art flew first class to Colorado, and when he commented what a comfortable, easy flight it was, Becky, Melissa, Brad and I all gave him a noisy raspberry. The kids laughingly gave him a vivid account of our own travels: the flat tire we had in the middle of a cloudburst, the friendly ranchers who arrived to help us, the ghastly run-down motel that reminded me of the movie *Psycho*, the mosquito war at Yellowstone. The day before we were due to depart, while I was packing, I was thinking what fun it would be to have Art with us on the trip home.

That last night in Aspen, when Art came home from his meeting, the first words out of his mouth were, "You won't believe this…"

"Stop!" I said. "Don't say anything else, let me guess. You just had a phone call. There is an important meeting you must go to, so you have to fly out tomorrow instead of traveling with us. Right?"

He looked surprised. "How did you guess?"

I just smiled, a bit sadly, I must admit.

The next morning, Art had just enough time to visit Mesa Verde with us, before we dropped him off at the Durango airport for his flight to D.C.

As we left the airport, I flipped on the radio to our favorite rock music station and shouted over the music, "O.K. kids, I'm taking orders. Where shall we go next?"

Now, two weeks later, Nashville was our last night on the road. The next day we would be back in Oak Ridge. Becky drove her two-hour afternoon shift after lunch, and then, in mid-afternoon I took over the wheel as we headed toward Nashville. It can be confusing to watch for signs of motels, and then suddenly be ready to exit the freeway, so I wanted to be doing the driving as we got closer to town.

We were in luck. As we approached Nashville, the first exit advertised three motels. I turned off, and headed for the first motel. "No rooms available, Ma'am. Don't y'all know there's the Grand Ole Oprey this week?"

I pulled out and tried the next two motels but had the same answer. Back to the interstate we went, and drove east, exiting wherever we saw a motel sign. Finally, an hour or so later, at a Holiday Inn, there was a vacancy. The kids waited in the car, while I registered, and then drove into the parking garage.

The kids could see how exhausted I was. "Mom," Becky said, "you are so tired, go lie down and we'll unpack the car and bring everything to the room."

"You angels," I sighed, and didn't argue as I lay down on the bed. We had already had our supper, a picnic of sandwiches and apples at a roadside park, so there was no need to drag myself downstairs to eat. As soon as the kids had brought in the luggage, we piled on the beds, clicked on the TV and ate cookies as we watched a movie.

Feeling refreshed the next morning, we went downstairs for breakfast, eager to be on the road to home. I sat there sipping coffee when the kids finished and asked to be excused. "Mom," Melissa said, "Why don't you sit and have another cup of coffee. We can pack everything up and get the car loaded. Then when you come upstairs, you won't need to stop and pack." Becky and Brad nodded approval of this suggestion.

"You darlings," I said.

They took the room key and left.

I finished my coffee and took the elevator to the third floor. As I stepped off the elevator, I suddenly realized that I didn't know what our room number was. I only held the key briefly, just after I registered, but then I handed it to Becky while I drove up the garage ramp. She unlocked the door to our room, to let us in, and afterwards the kids urged me to rest while they unloaded the car. They made several trips back and forth to the car, while I lay on the bed taking it easy. I had never really looked at the room number the evening before when we checked in.

"Oh well, it won't be hard for me to find our room," I thought. " I will just go along the corridor and knock on every door I come to. It shouldn't take long."

There was a long central corridor, with rooms on both sides. At one end of that main corridor, there was a short corridor The two corridors were in the shape of the letter "T". I started at one end of the central corridor, knocking on every door. When I reached the short corridor at the other end, I turned the corner and knocked in the doors of the rooms on that short hallway. Only a few of the rooms were still occupied, and I realized that it was late, around 9:30 A.M., and most of the people had already checked out. I knocked on every door on that floor, and I was puzzled when the kids did not answer my knocking.

"Strange," I thought, "Oh well, I'll keep trying."

I began again, just as I had started, knocking on every door, in exactly the same order I had followed the first time.

Only a few people in the occupied rooms answered my knock, looking uneasily at me the second time I knocked.

Where were my kids? I was beginning to feel desperate. A third time I walked back quickly to the end where I started each time, and began knocking again. This time, the people in the occupied rooms that opened, had the chains on, as they cautiously peered out at me. Clearly, I was some kind of nutcase, to be handled with caution.

Suddenly, to my relief, I saw a workman carrying a ladder into one of the rooms. I hurried to the room, asked to use the telephone, and he let me in. When the front desk answered my call, I asked which room Mrs. Arthur Upton was registered in. Soon the answer came back. "Sorry, Ma'am, we don't have innyone by that name registered here."

"Wait a minute! You are wrong, I know you have a Mrs. Upton here. She came in with three children around 8 o'clock last night! Look again!"

"No, Ma'am. We don't have innybody by that name registered here. Maybe she is sharin' a room with somebody else." There was a sly innuendo in this last comment. It didn't help my mood at all.

How could I be lost here in the Holiday Inn? Where are my kids? What should I do? Of course they are here. What a stupid jerk at the front desk. Can't he read? Do they hire illiterates here? I muttered to myself as I walked out past the, by now, very nervous workman up on the ladder. He had stopped working, and just stared at me, clutching a hammer in one hand. He watched me fearfully as I stalked out the door to the main corridor.

I continued to mumble to myself, "O.K, I'll do this one

more time. They'll answer this time, of course they will, Good God…must be going crazy, Now I'm talking to myself like a certified loony! Gotta stop this…think."

Quickly I walked back to my starting place, "knock, knock, knock…" I repeated my pattern, down the center corridor, turn right at the short corridor at the end, knock, knock, knocking my way to the end, and turn to the left. There was no response

"This is awful! Where are my kids? This is real life, this isn't a Hitchcock movie… That stupid jerk at the front desk… gotta go look at his book myself… "

I hurried to the elevator, and went downstairs to the front desk as fast as I could. "Look here, I know you have Mrs. Upton staying here. Look again…"

"Now, Ma'am, lookee here, I already checked it for you twicet before."

I stood there and thought back to my signing in the night before. Maybe I had writtten Mrs. Arthur C. Upton too close together. "Wait! Do you have a Mrs. Arthur Cupton staying here?"

" Why, yes, ma'am we shore do. Why izzen that innerestin' that you have two friends with such simular names, Upton and Cupton?"

I raced upstairs, dashed to the door of our room, pounded on the door with relief. The door opened a crack. The chain was on. "Oh, Mom, Mom are we glad to see you! Some crazy person has been knocking on the door, but each time we open the door, they have run away. It's been awful." I threw my arms around all three of the kids, heaving a sigh of relief.

Then I realized that our room was the very last room on the main corridor. Each time I started knocking my way down the corridor, I followed in the same pattern, so that ours was the last door on the main corridor. Each time, before the kids had answered my knocking, I had already turned the corner, and we had just missed each other.

I grabbed all three of my beloved kids and we all started to laugh.

"Gosh, Maw," Becky said, "You've been lost and found in the Holiday Inn.".…

The Enemies List

I t was never my intention to get a master's degree in Spanish. It was all an accident, and at times, a ghastly nightmare.

That first fall quarter, just for fun and to cheer myself up, I had gone over to the University of Tennessee at Knoxville and registered for a basic Spanish class. I liked the teacher and I enjoyed joking around with the kids in the class, a friendly bunch. It was a relief to discover that I still had a functioning brain. Yet Spanish was not something I wanted to stay with. Conjugating Spanish verbs was definitely not my ultimate goal in life.

My ultimate goal? "What a laugh that is," I thought to myself.

My ultimate goal had been snatched away the spring before, so there I was, just killing time in an elementary Spanish class, while I struggled to forget how painful it had been to give up my dream of going back to college for a Masters in Fine Arts. I had looked forward to teaching art and still have time for my own painting.

That spring, I had carried a portfolio of my work to the Fine Arts Department to talk to the chairman, Professor Buck Dowling, about applying for graduate school. The year before, I had enrolled in his painting workshop in Oak Ridge, and he had been enthusiastic about my work.

"Betsy, how nice to see you," he said, greeting me with a smile and a handshake. However, as soon as I told him I wanted to apply to his department, he said, "Don't bother to apply, we don't want any women in our department. And don't leave your portfolio here. We'll just jury your work out the door." Then, a smile as he added, "By the way, Betsy, I really like your work, so don't take it personally."

I didn't say a word, just looked at him, picked up my portfolio and walked out of the Fine Arts Department. I was numb with shock, too numb to feel the grief that came later. For years I had looked forward to being free to return to school. I had daydreamed about being able, finally, to really immerse myself in art, with time and the opportunity to explore new directions in my painting. My children were old enough now that I wasn't needed at home anymore, so I knew that I would be able to really concentrate on finally working to develop a career that offered me everything I wanted.

Before I went in to Buck's office, I remembered my concern that the work in my portfolio might not be good enough for the Fine Arts Department. Instead, nobody even wanted to look at my drawings and paintings. Was my work good enough? I would never know. It didn't matter anymore. I could feel a lump, hard and cold in my chest, so I sat down on a campus bench, and knew that the lump was my broken heart.

So there I was, still yearning to get a graduate degree in painting, yet knowing that that door was closed to me. When my beginning Spanish class ended, I still had not found another career that excited me, so I decided to continue with Spanish while I explored other departments and other possibilities. I went to the Spanish department and was assigned to Don Sánchez as advisor. A charming elderly Spaniard, retired from the University of Florida, he was now a popular visiting professor. He insisted on putting me into an Advanced Grammar and Composition class, despite my protests that I didn't know enough Spanish to do the work. He also assigned me to a Latin American poetry class and told me to go register as an Adult Special. When I asked what an Adult Special was, Don Sánchez's casual reply was, "Doan worry about that." So I just forgot about it.

Once Don Sánchez's class began, I immediately saw that I

was way out of my depth. All the other students were graduate students, and all were fluent in Spanish. Some were native speakers, some Spanish teachers, and others, returning Peace Corps volunteers from Latin America. I never talked to any of them, since my Spanish was so limited. They walked out of class, in twos and threes, all speaking Spanish at machine-gun speed.

The following semester, most of the same graduate students were also enrolled in my Latin American poetry class. We were seated around a table in a seminar room, and again, as I spoke such poor Spanish, I contributed little to the discussions.

The first month of the class, the professor passed around a list of Latin American poets, and asked each of us to choose one. We were then assigned to research and compile a bibliography of that poet's work plus everything we could find that had been written about the poet. There was only one poet on the list whom I had ever heard of, Rubén Darío. I knew nothing about him, nor was I familiar with his work, but, as it was a familiar name, I spoke up, "Sir, I'd like to do Rubén Darío."

"Excellent," said Prof. Otero.

After class, riding down in the elevator, I commented that it sounded like an interesting assignment. Nobody answered. Then I heard someone say quietly, "Brownnose." Another muttered, "Show off." Behind me someone whispered, "Goddamn bitch."

I couldn't figure out what they were talking about, but I didn't ask. I knew they would just lapse into machine-gun Spanish if I said anything.

After class, I went to the cafeteria for a Coke, and as I paid the cashier, I saw one of the girls in the poetry class. I walked over and sat down at her table, "Anita, how do you like the poetry …" I started to say, but before I could finish the sentence, she stood up, looked at me angrily, then carried her tray across the dining room and sat down at a different table. "What is it with this damn university?" I muttered to myself. "First, because I'm the wrong sex, I am shut out of my life-long dream of an MFA, and a career teaching painting. Now, I find myself being treated like a leper by everyone in my Spanish classes. As far as I am concerned, I can either ignore the barbarians or I can get the hell out and do something else." The more I thought about it, the angrier I became.

I got up, carried my Coke and stalked into the Spanish department. Milly, the department secretary, was typing. She looked up, "Hey there, cutie. What's up? You look like you're about to start spittin' beebees."

"What's 'brownnose' mean?"

"Where'd you hear that? Who's been callin' who a brownnose?" She looked closely at me.

"I'm not sure. But someone muttered it in the elevator after class today. They all sounded pretty angry, and I just wondered why. Anyhow, never mind that. I just came in to tell you that I'm pulling out of the classes for next quarter."

"Pullin' out? What do you mean? Don't you want to finish your degree? If you think they are mutterin' stuff, they'll really have somethin' to mutter about if you quit, 'Hey, d'yall hear the news? Betsy can't hack the Master's degree. Too much for the pore li'l kid.'"

"Milly, stop. What do you mean don't I want to finish my degree? What's that about I can't hack the Masters? I'm not working on a degree. I just started Spanish classes for fun… only with this bunch, there sure isn't any fun …" I struggled to hold my tears back as I looked at her.

Milly stood, came over a put an arm around my shoulders, and led me over to a chair. "Sit down, dear, I don't want to shock you, but honey, you are a graduate student workin' on your M.A. in Spanish, no matter what you think you're doin'.

What'd you think Adult Special meant?"

"I just thought it meant I had permission to take an advanced class that I wasn't ready for and never should have let myself be talked into."

"But you did, sugar. And you did real good. I saw your grade point average. Now, go on home, and decide if you want to stick it to 'em or whether you want to drag home, with your tail tucked into your bee-hind."

Numb from the shock, I hugged Milly, "God, Milly, can you stand to have a tired, old graduate student give you a hug?"

The next quarter, I was again in a class with Don Sánchez. The course was to read and criticize *Don Quijote*. It was a book I had always planned to read in English, but had been put off by the size of the thing. Daunting as it was in English, in Spanish, it was terrifying. I opened the first page. My God, I could only recognize about three words on the entire page.

"Come on, you gotta stick it to 'em, baby." I said to myself. "Stand up straight, suck up that gut..." Now it was my father's voice telling me what to do first. I laughed momentarily as I remembered Daddy teaching me how to double up my fists and punch as hard as I could, whenever I got into a fight.

"O.K. Daddy, I'm doubling up my fists and I'm going to punch it to 'em as hard as I can."

The next day, I was prepared for the seminar. Warned that Don Sanchez would ask students to translate and comment on the first chapter, I had spent most of the day before with a dictionary, writing the definitions of all the unfamiliar Spanish words in the margin of each page.

We took our seats, and Don Sánchez looked around the table. He glanced at each student and welcomed us. He glanced at my book, opened to the first page, then, startled, he looked more carefully. "I wan you students to look at Betsy's book. There is a real scholar, see how she has annotated each page? That ees what you all mos learn to do."

I looked up, noticed the students all glaring at me, and immediately corrected Don Sánchez's misunderstanding, "Oh, Don Sánchez, I haven't annotated the text. All this writing in the margin is just the definitions of the Spanish words I don't know. The rest of the class doesn't have to do this, because they already know Spanish. They can read it without looking up every word!"

Don Sánchez looked dismayed and I noticed several students looking at him, trying to conceal their amusement.

An hour later, walking out of class, one of the women came up to me and said, "Hey there, I'm Lee Shaw. How'd you like to go get a cup of coffee, and let me show you how to read a novel in Spanish?"

"Wonderful!" I said. "And will you please define 'brown-nose' for me? It's not in my dictionary."

"Oh, you know that's what they've been callin' you, huh? Well, if you're going to pick one of the greatest of all Latin American poets, and you're willin' to do a fifty page bibliography on the man, no wonder everybody thinks you're a brown-nose, which just means trying to suck up to the teacher by doin' a lot of extra work. Why didn't you pick one of those other poets? Nobody writes anything about unknown poets, so we all did only about half page bibliographies on them. The students all think you're tryin' to show off how brilliant you are."

I laughed for the first time in months. "Brilliant! What a laugh! The only poet I ever even heard of was Rubén Darío. How did I know I'd wind up with fifty pages of bibliography? I didn't major in Spanish, and I've just been hanging on by my fingernails in every class I've taken, and nobody would even talk to me. Me, brilliant? What a crock!"

"Well, I'm glad I finally figured out that you're not our brilliant Spanish scholar." Lee and I began to laugh together.

She added, "Poor old Don Sánchez. He really thought he finally had him a real, honest to God scholar. Well, I guess I'll just have to tell the truth, and let everyone know that you're really pretty dumb, and they should all treat you like a special needs student. That ought to get you off their enemies list."

Lee and I carried our coffee over to a table by the window in the cafeteria and she had me open my copy of Don Quijote. "O.K., look here. All you need to do it pick out the noun and the verb in each sentence. Just underline them, and go on to the next sentence. Here, use my pencil."

"But what about all the rest of the sentence? What about all the descriptions of things?" I asked her.

"Look, you don't have time for all those adjectives and adverbs, they aren't worth a damn. All you want to know is who did what. When you get to know Spanish better, you can take a look at the adjectives and adverbs in a book. But to hell with them now." She sat back and grinned at me.

So I decided not to quit graduate school after all. For one thing, I never could find anything else that looked more interesting than Spanish, and besides, with a friend like Lee Shaw, I knew it would all be fun again.

Oh Shit!

My first year at the University of Tennessee began with my taking a beginning Spanish Grammar class. After I was denied admission to the Fine Arts Department's graduate program because they didn't want any women in their department, I was so heartbroken and depressed to see my dreams casually shot down by the Fine Arts chairman, that I just listlessly skimmed the university catalogue of courses to see what might be interesting to take. To me, it all looked so boring. Why would anyone want to read a boring page of text when they could have the joy of laying down a stroke of color that was the perfect touch! And to me, the smell of turpentine and oil paint was like food to a starving man.

Then, suddenly, I thought back to how much I had loved my Spanish classes, at Tombstone High School in Arizona, and later, the two semesters of Spanish I enjoyed in college where I was an Art major. However, so many years had gone by, and I retained so little of the Spanish grammar I had learned, that I decided to start all over in a beginning Spanish class.

Then, as I mentioned earlier in the story *The Enemies' List*, the next semester was a nightmare of finding myself in graduate level Spanish classes, snubbed by the other students yet somehow hanging on by my fingernails.

When the fall quarter came, I met with my advisor, Don Sánchez, and to my horror he told me that I was to be appointed one of the Graduate Assistants for that year. The thought of teaching a beginning Spanish class or of working as an assistant to one of the Spanish professors, who mostly spoke Spanish, terrified me.

"Oh now, doan you worry. You weel do a fine job and besides, get money for tuition." The dear old man burst into laughter at the expression on my face. 'Take away from that pretty face sotch fear!"

The next thing I knew, I was given an office to share with the other Spanish graduate assistants in an old house on Rose Avenue. When I looked at the shiny new set of office keys in my hand, I felt a rush of pride and excitement at this amazing new status symbol, dangling from my fingers. In addition to having an office, and a desk of my own to keep student records and to grade papers, there was a parking lot behind the building, a very scarce item in that area of Knoxville, where the university had encroached on the old residential neighborhoods. Our Rose Avenue parking space filled up quickly, and only the early birds got the worms behind our building. The freshman Spanish class I was assigned to teach met early in the afternoon, so I rarely managed to park behind our office. Even so, I was grateful for that schedule, as I was so nervous about teaching a subject I knew virtually nothing about, that I needed all morning to get up my nerve to walk through that door, face the students and pretend that I was capable of teaching them a subject I barely knew. Then, I was also glad that the class ended at 2, since I then had a couple of hours to recuperate from the trauma of teaching before I had to go home and cook dinner for the family.

Then one Wednesday morning in October, I had to get to U. Tenn early, to grade papers. The day before I had run into Martha Cauldwell at the Pine Valley Pharmacy. A friendly North Carolina girl, Martha was working on a Ph.D. in English literature, and I had met her when I first started taking classes. "Hey there, Bets. I'd love to share rides with you to U.T. any time it works out. It would be more fun to have company than jest drive alone."

"Great idea, Martha. As a matter of fact, tomorrow I have

to get there early to grade papers. Would you mind an early ride, say if I pick you up around 9?"

"Hey, honey! Perfect! I'll be looking forward to going together. Next time, I'll drive, O.K?"

Martha was ready when I stopped to pick her up on West Outer Drive. I sat there absorbed in the gorgeous view Martha's house had of the Cumberland Mountains in the distance, and the lush green valley in the foreground, both shrouded in mist that early in the morning.

"What a view you all have, Martha."

"Oh, thanks. Yeah, it is nice, when you stop to look at it. Isn't it funny how after awhile, you just don't think about things that once really socked you in the face?"

We got to Knoxville around ten o'clock, and I turned down Rose Avenue. "Yeah, I know, there's not a chance we'll find space behind my office, but we might as well try." Martha nodded. We both knew the parking problems in that big university that had outgrown the neighborhood.

"Wait! Holy Baloney! Martha! We have our choice of parking spaces. I don't believe it! The entire parking area is empty. Are we in luck!" I parked the car under the lovely big shade tree, said good-by to Martha, and arranged to meet at my office around 4o'clock to drive home.

It was a productive day. Nobody was in our Spanish office in the Rose Avenue annex, and I plowed through the work I had to do. After teaching my class, I met a couple of friends, had a Coke with them, and wandered back to my office to meet Martha and head on home. We met each other on the sidewalk and walked together to the parking space behind my office.

"What! Good Grief! What's happened to my car?" I burst out. There, parked just where I had left my pretty clean white car was a shape of a car totally covered with bird droppings, in a variety of colors: green, yellow, reddish brown with areas of bright red dripped over the base colors. When I walked over to touch it I found a hard crust of all those layers of bird droppings. The hot Tennessee sun had baked those layers of multicolored bird poop onto that clean white car. I looked up at the tree and saw the problem. The green berries that covered the tree, which I had noticed but paid no attention to, had matured into various degrees of ripening. The tree was now covered with multicolored berries, green berries, pale yellow berries, reddish brown or bright red. The tree was inhabited by a huge swarm of birds, all pushing and shoving to get at the best berries for that lovely warm Tennessee afternoon.

"Ah'm NOT riding in that mess with you!" Martha burst out. "What would folks think if they saw me ridin' aroun' in that horrible mess?"

"Good luck, then," I said. "I don't mind if you can get another ride. I'm not too thrilled with this myself." I scraped the bird droppings enough to see where to put the key, unlocked the trunk and grabbed out scrapers for snow. What a shock I had when I tried to scrape the crust off. It had hardened onto the finish of the car like cement that had set up. I worked on the windshield, then the rear window, and the side window on the driver's side to gain some degree of visibility. I worked, scraping with all my strength for a good hour and a half, but no amount of scraping could get off more than a few inches of the baked on bird poop crust. Meantime, muttering to myself, "No wonder nobody at the Rose Street office parked there today. They all knew about the tree and the ripe berries!" And while I was furiously working to create some visibility to enable me to drive home, Martha kept on insisting that she absolutely refused to be seen in that disgusting car. I had no idea what a self-centered pain in the neck she was and decided that was our first and last trip together.

I finally gave up scraping and we got into my formerly

clean white car, Martha complaining the entire time, ducking her head as we drove down Cumberland Avenue. When we got to the first intersection, stopped by the red light, I saw that none of the cars on either side of the street were moving. Drivers were doubled over laughing so hard at the sight of my multicolored bird poop car, that nobody could drive. Traffic came to a total standstill. Drivers and passengers were pointing to our crusty car, just laughing their heads off.

After a few minutes, I heard a police siren, and a police car came slowly into the intersection. I expected the two cops to get things moving in a hurry., and waited for them to get out of the squad car and control the traffic jam. Instead, when they got out of the squad car, and walked over to me to see what the trouble was, both cops took a look, then doubled over with laughter, they just stood there in the middle of the intersection unable to move. Finally, when the traffic lights changed, some of the first cars moved on, but as cars further back in line drew closer and saw our car, new traffic jams were the result, with additional drivers unable to drive, they were laughing so hard. More squad cars arrived, and each new pair of police officer doubled over with laughter at the sight of my car. Meanwhile, poor Martha was cowering on the floor, with a scarf covering her face, she was so afraid someone she knew might see her in that multi-colored bird poop encrusted car.

Finally, one of the police officers came over to me, and said, "Lady, you jest have to get that work of art movin'. Now doan y'all drive too fast, or you're shore to cause an accident, but just try to keep movin'. These cars are backed up for a mile or two. We're gonna run a police escort to get you through these lights and onto I-40. That way, y'all kin git back home to Oak Ridge.

Poor Martha never saw it, but there we drove along, just like the president or the governor of Tennessee, with two squad cars in front, lights flashing and sirens blaring and two police car behind us.

That was the only time I ever stopped traffic in a city. I said to Martha, hoping to jolly her out of her embarrassment, "Well, Martha, now we both know the recipe for how to get to be the center of attention. Just find a tree, wait until the berries are ripe..."

The Tennessee Waltz

One of my first interests in Oak Ridge was working to establish an Arts Center. Our immediate goal was to attract artists as well as people who were interested in art, willing to work together to raise money and ultimately construct a building. We hoped to be able to have studio space for classes or workshops and exhibition space. These were long-term goals, and we all knew they would require serious fund-raising efforts.

The group decided to offer a Beaux Arts ball that we hoped would become a popular annual event. With different themes for each annual ball, and prizes for costumes that were creative and that expressed the different themes, the arts committee hoped to publicize the Arts Center and also make enough of a profit to establish a savings fund for our long-term goals. We were optimistic that we could attract a large group of party-lovers and ballroom dancing lovers who would return every year.

The theme of the first Beaux Arts Ball was Science Fiction and Fantasy. Neither Art nor I had gone to costume parties before, even though we went to many big dances in college. In Oak Ridge we had joined two dance clubs, one that only did Latin American dances, so the prospect of a costume party was very appealing to both of us. I loved the challenge of designing costumes that exemplified the theme of science fiction. Here was the opportunity to play around with costume ideas, which I also enjoyed when I designed Halloween costumes for our kids.

Going to the dance as robots or planets was out, as far as I was concerned. Too uncomfortable, I thought, visualizing boxy and cumbersome shapes piled on our heads. Since we

both loved to dance, I also was determined to design costumes that we could move around in easily, and do a rumba
or two, if we had the chance. I was also busy with our young
family, so I wanted to come up with costumes that would not
take too much time to make.

My "A-ha!" moment occurred when I was driving past
the dry cleaner. I stopped, went in, and asked if I could buy
two of the big cedar garment bags that were popular in those
days for storing out-of-season clothes. The bags were strong,
made of many layers of heavy cedar-smelling paper, not easily torn and durable enough to jitterbug in with no fear that
the costume would disintegrate.

Next I stopped at the nearest drug store and bought a
couple of candy bars, on my way home.

I cut holes in the center of the top and sides of each bag
for our heads and arms to extend through comfortably. Then
I pulled out charcoal, paints and brushes. I lay the two cedar
bags on the ping-pong table, and set to work. On one bag,
with a charcoal stick, I lightly sketched a Milky Way candy
bar, and on the other bag, I drew a Mars Bar. I then mixed
the colors of each candy bar wrapper, and in half an hour, our
costumes were finished.

The evening of the party, Art and I were delighted to
discover that our costumes were very comfortable and easy
to dance in. We danced every dance, with each other and
with friends, as well. Then, the young male vocalist started to
sing *My Tennessee Waltz*, and I fell in love. It was love of the
song, which I still love, it was love of the evening, wearing
crazy costumes and feeling like a child again, it was love of
the adorable young man who sang. He was very young, with
curly black hair, a wonderful smile with dimples and flirta-
tious blue eyes.

Suddenly, the judging of the costumes was to be announced, and the music stopped. Art and I were delighted

when we won the prize for the most original costumes.

Today, the flavor of Milky Ways or Mars Bars is still mixed up with the memory of hearing *My Tennessee Waltz*. The result is the taste of my childhood's favorite candy, and the memory of feeling like a child again, as we danced in our paper costumes, mixed together with the lovely sound of that young vocalist singing *My Tennessee Waltz*.

Of Mice and Kids in Oak Ridge

Most people seem to associate Oak Ridge, Tennessee with the word "Atom." Oak Ridge was that mysterious place was where those "crazy scientists" worked on the atom bomb during World War II. Even today, 69 years after VJ Day, the end of the war in the Pacific, the word "Atomic" or "Atom" continues to be associated with Oak Ridge.

The title of a recent book, *The Girls of Atomic City* by Denise Kierman, is easily recognized as being about Oak Ridge just from that word "Atomic". Often, when asked "Where was that town where you lived in Tennessee?" I answer, "Oak Ridge, you know, the atomic city…" and they immediately get it. "Oh yeah, where they built the A bomb."

But for me, the word "mice" or "mouse" conjures up my memories of our life in Oak Ridge, never the word atom or atomic. So much of the peacetime research carried on in the Biology Division, where Art worked, was done using mice. During the years when he worked with Jacob Furth, the two of them began a long-term study of the affects of radiation on mice. Following the war, and the bombings of Nagasaki and Hiroshima, this was a subject of enormous interest.

Mice were subjected to radiation in varying amounts and at different ages, using mice that were specially bred to be as similar, genetically, as it was possible in order to minimize possible differences in reactions. After this, the mice were allowed to live out their life spans, and after they died, they were autopsied and the results analyzed. The study continued until all the mice died. Important information was gained by this study, among which were proof of increased leukemia and other kinds of cancer. Oak Ridge attracted scientists from all over the world, interested in the ongoing results of this study.

There was another major discovery that Art and Jacob Furth played an important role in. A scientist named Ludwig Gross reported that his research indicated that leukemia in mice could be transmitted by using cell-free filtrates of tissue taken from mice with leukemia, then injecting it into baby mice within a few hours after birth. This would cause them to develop leukemia later in life.

Gross was open about his experiment, but nobody was able to duplicate the same results, so he was labeled a charlatan by other scientists. Both Art and Jacob were gifted with scientific curiosity, and neither one of them was satisfied by the accusations against Gross. The two agreed to invite Dr. Gross to come to Oak Ridge and allow him to duplicate his findings. They suspected that other scientists might have overlooked some detail of Gross's experiment.

Gross went to Oak Ridge, and worked in the Biology lab replicating his experiment while Art and Jacob took careful notes as they observed his technique. Then, Jacob Furth insisted that Gross leave Oak Ridge, return to his own lab, and let Furth and Art watch the results. Gross had to agree that they would not tell him anything until the experiment was over.

As the months went by, Gross started telephoning Art and Furth demanding to know what was going on with the baby mice he had injected. Each time, Art had to remind him that he would be told only when the results were all available. Poor Ludwig Gross had been so traumatized by other scientists labeling him a faker and liar that he began to accuse Art and Jacob of cheating him. He became suspicious that the two of them were plotting against him, and planning something underhanded.

However, at the end, Art and Jacob Furth were able to report to the scientific world that Ludwig Gross's theory was correct. The results of his work with the mice in Oak Ridge clearly proved that the mouse leukemia virus could be transmitted to newborn mice. Art told me that the other scientists ignored Gross's insistence that the newborn mice must be injected within a limited period of time post-partum. Art came home, with a big smile when he told me that he and Jacob Furth had told Ludwig Gross that his work was an extremely important contribution to the field of knowledge about leukemia.

I understood Art's fascination with research. Briefly, as an undergrad in college, I had a vacation job in the Psychology department running rats through mazes. I loved the rats and mice I worked with. Even so, I often resented the fact that Art spent more of the weekends with his beloved mice than with the kids and me. Art's mice were a formidable rival for me, although I rationalized that mice were preferable to another woman as rivals for his affections. It was better to have him come home smelling like mice than like Chanel No. 5.

One evening, when our children were still in grade school, Art brought home a large cage with two pregnant female mice. "It will be fun for the kids if they can watch the mice when they give birth." he told me. "We will have a chance to see the maternal instinct that females are born with."

We all had great fun watching the two little mice running around in the big cage, their bellies filling out as the pregnancies went on.

Then came the big day, except that it turned out to be the big night. Both females gave birth while we were all sound asleep, so none of us was able to watch them give birth. Then at breakfast, we saw that our family had taken a jump in size with two proud mouse moms, each with five tiny naked pink babies. The kids and I were terribly disappointed not to have seen the mice being born, but they became the center of attraction for all of us.

In reality, we soon discovered there was only one true mother mouse. One of the new mouse mothers absolutely refused to have anything to do with her babies. When they yowled for food, she ran squeaking to the opposite end of the cage, and sat there, refusing to feed her litter. The other mother mouse was a most attentive mother, feeding her litter, and cuddling with them. After her babies were asleep, she ran to the abandoned litter and licking them and nuzzling them, she proceeded to nurse the hungry babies abandoned by their mother. A pattern emerged: one mother seemed totally lacking in maternal instinct, while the other mother was so maternal that for the next several weeks, until the babies were ready to eat kibble, she cared lovingly for both litters of baby mice.

"So, Art, there's a nice bit of research for you," I kidded. "Are you going to write a paper refuting the theory that females all have innate maternal instincts? This little party-girl mouse is just like Karen on Pine Lane. The minute her cleaning woman walks in, Karen walks out and spends the day as far as she can get from her kids, poor little things."

Our mother mice and the babies returned to the lab, but mice remained a part of our lives. Once we started having pet snakes, Art brought mice home, and they were served tender and juicy to our new pets. Loving mice as we all did, we soon learned to look the other way during snake snacktimes.

Nineteen years of living with mice in one way or another has firmly established Oak Ridge in my mind as the Mouse Town, and not as the Atomic City, although I must admit that it is not as catchy a sub-name for the place that helped to make the A-bomb.

Epilogue: Bad Blood

I will close with a story of an incident told to me by Ezra, Willie's gentle old grandfather, who used to mow the field around our cottage. He told me the story because it happened to a young man we both knew. Ezra knew I would share his sadness over the tragedy.

The title is <u>Bad Blood</u>. I have written it as though it were told to me by one of the country people, since it is not my story. It gives a glimpse into a culture and belief system that at first seemed foreign to me. However, we have many of the same kinds of preconceived prejudices about strangers living in our own culture, so that the story mirrors our own kind of cruelty to those whom we persist in seeing as "others" in our midst, and whom we never really accept.

When Petey come home with Wilma, folks in the valley was surprised. Oh, ever'body knowed he was sweet on some gal up to Crossville way, but didn't nobody know exactly who she was. He'd just take off after he'd git off work at the lumber mill, go on by his pa's house, take the pick-up and head down the road. None of his folks wanted to ask Petey too much, he wouldn't a told 'em nothin' if they had of. He was always a secret kind of boy, went his own way without a lot of talkin'. Some of his old buddies would kind of tease him about havin' to go up on the mountain to git it, but he never said nothin' back, just kinda smiled some.

The week before Petey drove back with Wilma, someone seen him workin' around the old Jenks cabin up by the creek. Old man Jenks died there couple of years back and ain't nobody been near the place since. Some said the old man had died havin' a fit, foamin' at the mouth, eyes rollin' around in his head. Others said he had a hex on him, and folks was scared of gittin' anywheres close by his cabin. The place was kinda run down, front door hangin' off and most of the windows was broke by kids throwin' rocks. But there was Petey, and looked like he was fixin' to move in after he done some repair work. Folks said it was about time he got hisself his own place, and others thought it was time he got hisself a wife. Course then, we was all wonderin' about that there Crossville girl we heard he was keepin' company with.

So for us folks that knowed about the Crossville girl friend, it wasn't no surprise when he come drivin' along in the pick-up lookin' pleased with hisself. Sittin' over close to him was a scared-lookin' rabbity kinda girl. But that was jest how she looked from where me and Ezra was standin' by the gas pump out front of Billy McCoy's store. Petey pulled the pick-up over, and leaned out the window, "This here is Wilma. Me and her got married yesterday."

"Well, howdy and welcome to you, missus," Billy said as we all walked over to meet her. Ezra and me both tole her welcome to the valley.

She give us a shy smile, and said, "Pleased to meet you" to Billy and Ezra and me. Her voice was soft as a quail feather, when she spoke. Funny how that soft voice kind of matched how she looked back then. She was a right purty little gal, maybe too skinny for some, but with a soft, gentle look about her. Her blond hair was long and hangin' straight down her back, but what I can't forgit is them sky blue eyes of hers. She had the kind of big eyes that looked right at a person, clear and trustin'. Put me in mind of a doe I killed last year, and the way that doe done looked in my eyes, afore I shot her. Wilma's eyes was like that, like she knowed you wasn't goin' to hurt her.

When Petey was introducin' us to her, she set there, near as close as she could git to him. "We're goin' to live up at Jenks' old place," he said. "Ain't nobody wantin' it, so I done some fixin' up." Then, lookin' kinda embarrassed, Petey put the pick-up in gear and drove up the valley road.

"Ain't that a surprise," Ezra commented. "I wonder if the Harling's knowed their boy was goin' to git married. Petey's a nice young feller, and bout time he settled down."

After that, folks started coming down to Billy's store, to find out was that Petey with a woman in his truck. Billy done a heap a business that day, what with folks actin' like they was there just because they needed flour or some eggs or a couple onions. But nobody knowed for sure where Wilma was from, nor who her people was. Jest that she was from up on the Cumberland Plateau, near Crossville.

Petey and Wilma moved into the Jenks' cabin and pretty soon they was curtains hangin' at the windows. Petey got him some leftover paint from the lumber mill and painted the door of the cabin. And folks up the valley walkin' past to come down to Billy McCoy's store said they seen Wilma diggin' her a flower garden and settin' a big tin with petunias right next to the door.

Folks stayed away at first, thnkin' to let the two of them git used to married life. Mostly, that's what the valley does, even when it's one of our own young 'uns. Then, long about the second month, valley folks start droppin' in on a new-married couple, to carry over some kind of gift, like preserves, some fresh eggs, a pan of cornbread or some needlework. If it's a feller what likes his nip, someone with a still up the valley will likely carry him a bottle of sploe.

All the valley neighbors was startin' to drop by Petey's place. We was all curious to see what Wilma was like, and they was a few who wanted to see was she carryin'. And it ain't a nice thing to say, but not a few was sorry to see she was flat as a pancake and it looked like Petey wasn't forced into marrying her after all. It looked to me like that the ones who claimed it had to of been a shotgun weddin', was mostly folks like Mamie Ebbets, her having three grandbabies and both her girls livin' at home, neither one married. Mamie had her eye on Petey before he brung Wilma home, and I reckon she hoped he might start keepin' company with her daughter, Doreen, and be a father to Doreen's two babies. They was more'n one valley woman eyein' Petey. He was a hardworkin' young feller, with a good, steady job over at the lumber mill.

Wilma probably didn't ever know how folks was gossipin' about her and Petey. Or maybe she guessed, but didn't seem to pay it no never mind. She acted right happy to meet her new neighbors and the other valley folks. Ever time company dropped in to visit, Wilma welcomed them in her soft voice. She brung out coffee and hoecake or cookies, and asked folks to set down and rest awhile. Some of us went back more'n once, she was that friendly. Course, Petey was off workin' at the lumber mill, so she like to've been real lonely livin' in a strange place.

Friendly as folks was to Wilma, back then, they wasn't anybody found out who her folks was. Come to think on it, none of us even knew what her last name was, afore she and Petey done got married. Not even her next door neighbor, Jane Purdy.

Wilma and Jane got real close. They was both near the same age, both new married and both lookin' for a friend. Janie was married to Seth Purdy. He was old enough to be her daddy, with a passel of kids from his first marriage, and some said only married Janie so she could raise the two littlest ones. Seth Purdy was a hard man. He'd worked in the coal mines over in the Cumberlands for near on to twenty-five years until they closed, and he come home to the valley with a bad cough. Mostly he set on the porch drinkin' and yellin' at Janie and little Todd and Sonny. When he was sober, he had him a smile that could charm the skin off a snake. Folks said they was a few more of Seth's kids here and there in the valley that nobody said nothin' about.

But, like I was sayin', Janie and Wilma got to be real good friends. Wilma had that soft, gentle way about her that folks liked, and especially the young'uns in the valley. First it was Janie's step-kids, little Todd and Sonny that started goin' over to visit Wilma when she was workin' in the yard, or hangin' out laundry. Then. pretty soon, the other kids began to go visit Wilma. We'd see her settin' there on the front stoop at times, with a bunch of little ones on the ground around her, and she'd be tellin' them stories while she set there, doing some needlework. She was real good at stoppin' tears, and fixin' up bloody knees, too. We got used to seein' her walkin' down to Billy's store with somebody else's young'un holdin' her hand, and the other mothers was just as happy to let her take care of them little ones. So they'd tell 'em to go on over to Wilma's if they was too busy to fool with their own kids.

Things was pretty much the same even after Wilma and Petey had their baby girl that following year. Folks still stopped to visit and send their little ones over to see her. And even with her bein' busy with her own baby, May Sue, Wilma still had time for huggin' and story-tellin' with other folks' kids. It was nice to see how that skinny, scaredy-lookin' little gal had fit right into the valley. She had fattened up and got right purty after she married Petey.

Then Granny Baker's daughter, Lettie, come home to visit and we found out about Wilma's family. Lettie was livin' up near Crossville, and some of her husband's kinfolk livin' near Wilma's folks knowed the truth.

Wilma's famiy had bad blood. Nobody knowed for sure how the bad blood was started. Maybe it was because her great-grandma was part Cherokee, who some said was a healer, but others said maybe she was a witch. Maybe it was somethin' her grandpa done. These things is hard to know.

But when the valley heard about Wilma, folks just knowed they wasn't a thing could be done about it. Bad Blood can't be changed. Everybody knowed that Wilma was bound to go wrong, so valley folks just waited to see. They stopped goin' by to visit her, and they kept all the young'uns away. Even Janie stopped goin' over next door to see her. And when Wilma walked down to Billy McCoy's store, carrying May Sue, folks turned away, pretendin' not to see her, so as not to talk to her. Folks still stopped to talk to her when Petey was with her, but they all felt real sorry for Petey marryin' a woman with bad blood, he bein' from a family with good blood.

And that's the thing about good blood, it don't matter much what you do, long as the family has good blood. Like Petey's brother Jake doin' time for manslaughter up to Brushy Mountain State Prison, and his sister run off with that preacher man who come here a few years back to preach at that revival, both of them married with kids, of course. But folks figure Petey's brother will go straight when he gits out and nobody thinks too much about his sister breakin' up a marriage. She is going to turn out jest fine, her bein' good blood and all.

But even though Granny Baker's daughter Lettie, said nobody never heard nothin' too bad about Wilma's family, even bad blood and all, folks knowed they was bound to go bad. So the valley just watched and waited for Wilma's bad blood to make her go wrong.

She began to change, mostly back to what she was like at first. She got thin again, and had that rabbity scared look on her face when she walked to Billy's store. And that spring nobody seen her plantin' her flowers like she done before. Petey went on the same, workin' at the lumber mill and comin' home to Wilma and the baby. But he never said nothin' to nobody about leavin' Wilma all alone, and sometimes we seen her with red eyes, when we'd pass by their cabin. Then some folks said they seen Seth Purdy over to Wilma's a few times, talkin' to her when she was hangin' out laundry. But nobody paid it no mind, him being a near neighbor and all.

Last week Wilma took the baby, May Sue and run off with Seth. Hit ain't no surprise at all to the valley. Everbody knowed she would go wrong, her with her bad blood.

Author Biography

Betsy Perry Upton is an Army Brat who grew up enjoying the Gypsy life of moving to new places. A lifelong love of drawing and painting led her to a major in art at the University of Michigan. Later, after changing fields, she completed graduate studies in Spanish Literature at the University of Tennessee and New York University. Her career includes teaching courses in Latin American Art and Culture, developing educational workshops for the Puerto Rican community on Long Island and translating books on art. She and her husband now live in Santa Fe, NM.